Frantic to Kill - Text c
Cover Art by Emmy I

C000258547

All Ri

FRANTIC TO KILL

EMMY ELLIS

CHAPTER ONE

Langham was on the late shift at his 'new' job. The weather had taken a wet turn, raining on and off for the past few days. The conditions these graveyard people worked in were atrocious, but he supposed the summer months made up for the bad ones. He glanced at his watch, pressing the side light button to illuminate the screen. Half an hour and he could go home. He had to admit that doing one shift—and only one—per day meant he wasn't as tired, that he had time to actually live.

Going undercover was weird. In a way, he'd been looking forward to returning to work after the Caribbean shite, except at the station or on the streets where he was in the thick of it, where he knew the procedure, which would have given him some sense of normality, of knowing how to deal with things. In the graveyard it was like a new career—one he wouldn't have chosen in a million bloody years. Standing on the periphery, watching people grieving as their loved ones were lowered into the ground, wasn't anything he'd choose to do. Still, he'd said he'd go undercover, and he had.

He'd been at it for a while. At the time the chief had asked him, he'd grabbed the chance to do something different, but now? Fuck, the monotony of his duties might end up reducing him to switching his mind off.

He couldn't afford for that to happen.

He had to be alert, to keep an eye out for unusual comings and goings, or listen for snippets of conversation that led to him knowing if other graveyard staff were working with the criminals.

Nothing so far.

But last night was a bit odd.

Yeah, now he came to think of it again, it was.

Some bloke had stood outside the cemetery, staring through the iron railings that posed as a fence. Stupid, because it wasn't that high—maybe five feet—and anyone could jump over if they felt like it. Langham had observed him surreptitiously for a bit, but the man hadn't done anything much except stand there. Or so he'd thought at the time. But what if that bloke had been watching him? What if he knew Langham was new and needed to check him out?

Shit.

Langham got his phone out, hiding it behind one of the front panels of his jacket so it didn't get wet. He texted the information to DI Fairbrother now he was SIO on the case, adding a description as best he could remember. Big man. Wide, tall. Short hair—crewcut, perhaps.

He paused to cast his mind back. A streetlight had shone on the figure, shrouding him in an orange glow that could have been classed as sinister if Langham were of a fearful disposition. Seeing as he saw people standing beneath lampposts all the time, it hadn't bothered him, but that face... No, he wasn't your average-looking fella.

He added to the text, telling Fairbrother he'd contact him again if the man came back. He pressed 'send' then slipped his phone into his pocket. There was work still to be done, and if the old man who was in charge of this place came along unexpectedly and caught him using his phone, Langham suspected it'd be grounds for instant dismissal.

He knelt on the soft, damp grass, reaching out to pull some dying petals from a wilting flower. Ignoring the gravestone and the words on it—he couldn't afford to let emotions cloud his mind—he thought about his options. Another fortnight at this gig, he reckoned, then he could go back to normal duty. Sod all was going on here except what was *supposed* to go on—folks being buried, graves being dug, and people visiting their beloveds.

He had to admit the serenity of the place had its merits. It gave him time to ponder shit he didn't usually have time for.

Something crackled.

He shot his head up, peering through the gloom. That man was there again, staring through the railings a couple of hundred metres away. Standing, Langham acted nonchalant, as if he were anyone other than a police officer.

That crackle sounded closer, though.

He turned his head left, surveying his surroundings, like he did when giving the graveyard the final once-over prior to securing it for the night. The crackle came again, behind him this time, and he was torn between spinning to face whatever was there or keeping tabs on the man at the railings.

He opted to spin.

One of his 'work' colleagues stood there. Mark, a bloke of about thirty-five. Hands stuffed in his pockets, he smiled at Langham, the hem of his beanie covering his eyebrows.

"What the fuck?" Langham let out a laugh that sounded as if he were spooked. "You shit me up then. What are you doing here?" He shifted his position so he was side-on to Mark, enabling him to check if the railing man was still there.

He was.

"I thought I'd do a stakeout." Mark shuffled from foot to foot. "You know, since those men are going missing again." He shrugged. "I wanted to see if *they* came back, the ones who dumped bodies." He nodded, gaze going in the direction of the railing man. "And him—what's that all about? Who stands at the fence when it's getting dark? Why doesn't he just come in if he wants to visit someone?"

"Christ knows," Langham said. "Maybe it's too painful. He might be getting up the courage to come inside." He made a show of looking at his watch again. "But he'd better hurry up. I'm locking the gates in five minutes. I ache like a bitch and need a bath then bed."

"Yeah." Mark stared at the bloke. "I know how that feels."

"Still, it's a job, eh?" Langham walked towards the curving pathway that skirted the grass. He wanted to be on firmer ground if something kicked off. He didn't know Mark that well. For all he knew, Mark could be a part of this.

Mark followed. On the path, he took a small Thermos from the inside of his jacket then hunkered down to pour a cup of something steaming. "Here." He held up the cup. "Bit of a warmer for you."

Langham's mind went into overdrive. Mark could be genuine, just some man offering a hot drink, but the bloke over at the railings had him thinking the two of them were a tag team.

I've seen too much during cases. Gives me ideas.

"This job," Mark said. "Wish I didn't have it sometimes. Creepy. As. Eff."

Langham laughed and took the drink. The scent of coffee had his mouth watering. The heat from the cup warmed his hand. "So you worked here when the bodies were dumped?"

Get information before you take a sip.

"Yeah, the tail end of it." Mark stood then gulped straight from the flask.

Can't be drugged then.

"I'd like to say that fella over there was one of the dumpers, but I can't." Mark's breath gusted in a dark-grey plume. The weather couldn't seem to make up its mind, mild one minute, cold the next. "Too bulky. The one I saw was thin. Fucking weirdo. His mate was, too. Mind you, years have passed, and we all put a bit of beef on, don't we."

"So what happened?" Langham gave in and drank some coffee. The liquid spread a lovely heated line down into his belly. "Can't say I'd want to carry on working here if I'd seen anything myself."

Mark gestured to the railings. "That man has fucked off."

Langham glanced over. *Thank God he's gone.*

"Anyway," Mark said. "I was on this shift. By myself, like you. I was inside a grave I'd dug with the digger earlier. You know, making sure it was deep enough, pressing the internal walls so the earth was a packed in tight. I'd propped a shovel against a tree beside the grave opening, and I heard this man." He paused, probably seeing it all in his mind. "He said, 'You'll be needing this shovel

6

a while longer'. Well, I crapped myself, didn't I. I remember a twig cracked, and there was the shuffle of footsteps. I'd been about to climb the ladder to get out, see."

The images that accompanied Mark's tale flooded Langham's head. It wasn't difficult to visualise the scene—he'd been in the same position digging a grave once or twice himself.

"So I had to find out who I was dealing with before I got out," Mark went on. "'Who's there?' I said. 'Never you mind', he said. The footsteps came closer, and the shape of the man moved. He picked up the shovel. Speared it into the grave. It landed right beside me. I looked up and made out a bloke in a black raincoat, the belt tight at the waist. He had a baseball cap on, the brim pulled low, and dress trousers and pointy-toed leather shoes." He shuddered. "I remember thinking: Who wears shoes like that?"

That was odd. A baseball cap coupled with dress shoes? The raincoat, too. Like the man was purposely dressing to freak people out. Langham frowned, thinking what kind of person it had been. A snob? Someone with a bit of money?

Mark finished his coffee. Langham did the same then passed the cup over.

"Cheers." Mark screwed it back on the flask and furrowed his brow. "He told me to dig and in no uncertain terms said that if I didn't, there'd be trouble." He laughed bitterly. "Like I could refuse with what looked like a gun pointed at me."

Langham hadn't seen that in any of the reports. "Did you tell the police?"

"Um, nope."

"Why not?"

"Because it was better I didn't. He said if I did, they'd come back and get me. So I just dug deeper and kept going until he told me to stop. After I'd finished, he said I was to forget what I'd done, forget he'd been there. And it *was* a gun—he waved it at me once I'd climbed out of the hole—and I was fucked if I'd ignore him with that kind of threat. I went back to the tool hut and got ready to leave the graveyard, but I hadn't been able to resist one more look back as I'd locked the cemetery gates." He shook his head. "I wish I hadn't."

"What did you see?" Langham held his breath, praying Mark would give him something Fairbrother could use to catch these bastards.

"I peered through the iron bars and watched him and one other chuck a body in the grave. I was so torn between fucking off home and calling the police, but the man's threats... Jesus." He shivered and glanced about, chuckling quietly.

What, did he expect the man to turn up again?

"Did you see him after that?" Langham asked.

"No, I got Reginald to put me on permanent days. I couldn't come back here to work at dusk."

"Yet you're here now."

"Yeah, nuts, isn't it? But you're here, so..."

"You might be subconsciously dealing with guilt." Langham reminded himself that to Mark he was just another member of the public, not a copper. "I heard, going by what was in the papers and whatever, that the body-dumping stopped

8

anyway. But since men are going missing off the streets again... You might be feeling bad, thinking the graves will be messed with."

"It did stop, yeah. But now it's kinda brought it all back. What if they kill them, put them in here again?" Mark stared at the fence where their watcher had been. "And what if that man who'd stood there is new to their team? You know, getting a feel for the place? Fucking hell..."

"God knows," Langham said, "but I'm going home. You telling me all that has made me uneasy."

Mark grimaced. "Now I've told you, it's reminded me of what could happen. And that man by the railings... I'm leaving with you."

Langham turned and walked towards the little hut where they took tea breaks. Mark tailed him. Picking up a shovel he'd propped against the hut, Langham gave the graveyard a quick scan. He put the shovel inside, locked the door, then jerked his head to tell Mark he'd finished. They hurried to the gate, and on the other side, Langham closed it then secured the padlock.

Mark sighed. "That's exactly what happened that night. I locked up. Stared through this gate to where those men were." He pointed. "Over there. See that big tree?"

"I see it."

"That's where it happened."

"How come you didn't just leave this job?" Langham strode in the direction of where he'd parked his car. He stopped beside it and clicked

9

his key fob. The door release alarm bleeped, and he opened the driver's side.

"I thought about it, but when I looked for other jobs..." Mark paused. "Well, there weren't any. I've got shit GCSEs, no one's hiring."

"You need a lift anywhere?" Langham asked.

"Nah, my car's over there."

"Thanks for the coffee." Langham smiled over the roof of his car.

"'S'all right. See you around."

Langham waited until Mark had driven off then got inside, locking himself in. He rang Fairbrother, telling him everything.

"So you reckon that man staring through the railings could be them again?" Fairbrother asked.

"I don't know—and I won't know if he comes back either because I'm on the early shift tomorrow. Unless he checks the place out in daylight, too." Langham pressed his lips tightly together. "I'd advise putting someone on watch in a car if you haven't already. I'll nip into the station first thing to show you where he stands using Google Street View."

"Right. Anything else I need to know?"

"Not that I can think of. If something comes to mind, I'll let you know."

"You do that."

Langham drove home. This would be the first time since starting at the graveyard that he wouldn't be able to shut out the job. Mark had opened the floodgates.

The fucking case had his full attention now.

Back to normality then.

CHAPTER TWO

Oliver rolled over in bed, failing to get to sleep. He opened his eyes and checked the clock. Not even midnight yet.

He stared around his bedroom. How different it looked compared to in the daytime. Every shape seemed to have malicious meaning in the dark. The furniture became monsters, the corners shadowed areas where ghosts hovered. Roll on meek sunlight plaguing the curtain edges, another dreary day, and any semblance of night-time fear vanishing.

Lethargy had him heavy of body and sluggish of mind. If spirit had kept him awake, giving him information to help the police, it'd be worth feeling like this, but the buggers had been silent.

His usual walk to work would be a chore, something he could well do without come the morning. The effort—too much after hours of staring into the darkness. He'd use his new car instead, despite the clogged traffic that was bound to fill the roads.

Such as it was during these times, his mind wandered to the mundane. He'd do a proper supermarket shop in his lunch break; he had a list of shit he needed. He was getting right into cooking—he ate too many takeaways because of Langham's erratic work schedule, them meeting at the detective's of an evening to thrash out whatever they were working on.

Oliver was on standby, waiting for spirit to speak to him regarding the current case. He grinned at the name Langham was going by. Robert Briggs. It was obvious why a name change was needed. If those men came back to bury the bodies of used and abused homeless men in already established graves, Langham's real identity had to be undisclosed. He needed to gather as much information as he could before he went back to regular police duty. That had nearly been on the cards—if Langham hadn't spotted some weird bloke staring at him through the iron railings. He'd phoned Oliver about that earlier, seeing if spirit had spoken to him regarding it.

Things always went tits up. Oliver didn't know why he expected anything to run smoothly. He'd been lulled into a false sense of security when Langham had agreed to go undercover. How could he have thought nothing untoward was going to happen?

He laughed quietly and shook his head.

Always the fucking way.

He knew from experience that thinking was a bitch on hairy legs. Especially when he couldn't sleep without bad crap invading his dreams or he couldn't kip at all. Many a day since the Caribbean shite had seen him groggy, out of sorts, and generally so weary he could have done with sleeping through the day following a bad night. He'd got up for work regardless, though. And that place pissed him off. Being a glorified tea boy at the local newspaper had never been a career aspiration. Mind you, it was a job, and not many employers would give a man time off to go gallivanting around with the police, helping out on murder cases.

Bloody ulterior motive. They got inside scoops on cases.

Saying that, a new editor was taking over this morning. Seemed a nice chap, if a bit older than the last. Went by the name of Eamon King. And maybe he'd be better to work for than the previous editor. Eamon had a wife and kids, and he'd come across as kindly when he'd introduced himself, more the type of bloke Oliver wouldn't mind having a pint with when the workday was done.

Time will tell.

Eamon had agreed to Oliver having time off at a moment's notice if spirit spoke to him and he was needed on one of Langham's cases. *And* he didn't expect any snippets of information.

Silver lining.

CHAPTER THREE

The day seemed to have gone on forever. The sun had dragged its arse across the sky. Lethargic bitch. Best not to moan about it, though. Night-time was back again, shrouding the young man from the accusing or sorrowful stares of passersby.

He hunched deeper into his bright-red coat. It had seen better days. The stuffing had flattened, the outer material bore a few rips and scratches, and the removable hood had lost two of its buttons. At least he *had* a coat, one he'd pinched from the sale rack outside Debenhams when no one had been looking. Of course, he'd run like hell once the coat had been in his hand, legging it through the crowd of shoppers who didn't seem to have any urgency about them. Millers, that's what he called them. People who milled about without a care in the world.

He should be so lucky.

He leant against the underside of the bridge wall, darkness bringing the usual fears that gnawed his gut, and admitted picking a red coat hadn't been one of his better choices. Mind you, it wasn't really red now, more of a dull burgundy owing to the filth he'd picked up over the past year.

He stared out across the way, taking in the stench of the dirty river meandering beneath the bridge. The brown water reminded him of melted milk chocolate, the ripples ghosts blowing the surface instead of the wind. He stood on a path that ran alongside it, wide enough that he could stretch out his arms if he had a mind. Not that he could do *that* very often. Better to be curled into a ball. Invisible.

A fire blazed halfway down the path beneath the bridge, the tang of it sharp. A blackened piece of paper flew into the air, swirling in the breeze. The old man he'd made friends with—Pete his name was—had set it inside a rusty oil barrel, using newspaper and the dried-up sticks he always collected by day. The young man had latched on to him not long after he'd run away from home. Pete called him Kid and reminded him of his grandad. Kid had always felt comfortable around old people. They didn't hurt him. Didn't expect anything of him except good manners and respect. He could do that, *did* that for them—for anyone who gave a shit.

Unfortunately, not many people did.

Still staring out of the archway, he took in the bright lights of London, spots of white, yellow, and red. The London Eye was visible, something he dreamed of going on but couldn't afford the fare. Who had forty-odd quid just knocking around? He just about made enough money to eat, and on the days he didn't, the bins outside the many McDonald's provided scraps to fill his aching, empty belly.

There were people in that vast city who lived in warm houses and smiled a lot. He knew this utopia existed. He'd watched the telly. Saw what went on beyond the realms of his own existence. His reality, though, had been different. Mum, with her brown, broken teeth and stinging slaps, had a love affair with drugs. She took them, sold them, and spent the majority of her time off her head. He wasn't sure how she'd got into that kind of life—it had been all he'd known—but surely once upon a time she'd been happy. Clean.

Yeah, she had always looked dirty. Greasy blonde hair stuffed back into a ponytail, the skin of her face a sickly grey pallor that bled into the darker circles beneath her eyes. During the last few months of him being at home, her wrinkles had become deep and ravine-like. When she'd hit him, her eyes had bunched in spite, and those wrinkles reminded him of Grandad's ancient concertina.

Dad...he was another story. He loved the drink, loved the money the drugs brought in, and his fists turned to iron most days. His parents had never worked, although they said they did. Drug running was a lucrative business that had them on their toes, they reckoned, keeping them up long into the night. As far back as he could remember, people had knocked on their front door way past sundown, entering the flat along with the scent of outdoors and other, indefinable smells. Kid used to sit in the corner of the itchy hessian couch, springs bursting through the brown fabric to poke him in the arse. And he'd watched what had gone on, knowing the visitors would leave once they'd got what they'd come for—small transparent bags containing white power or what looked like dried grass.

Dad had been pissed most of the time, probably still was, and Mum was usually high.

Grandad had once said to them, "How you've never been robbed is anyone's guess."

Dad reckoned it was because he had a name for himself. No, folks wouldn't mess with him. Kid knew otherwise. Once a week a bloke arrived, his pristine suit marking him out as someone altogether different from the usual visitors. Mum

18

handed him money, and the man slapped her bony arse and told her that cash was what kept the sharks from their door. She used to titter at him, a sound that grated on Kid's nerves, and Dad laughed. The bloke's smile didn't reach his eyes, though, and Kid instinctually knew his father didn't like the man slapping Mum.

Grandad had tried to protect Kid, risking the slaps and fists himself, and towards the end when...yeah, towards the end, the old man had kind of given up. Once Grandad had gone, Kid had known he'd have to follow his big brother out into the city, leaving behind the filth and spite.

Entering a different kind of filth and spite.

He'd hoped to find his brother, gone a long time now, on the streets he walked day in, day out.

He hadn't found him.

He shook off the memories.

"Reckon it's about time the black van made its rounds," Pete said from behind him.

Something in the fire crackled, and a flurry of blackened paper specks sifted out into the open air. Kid watched them go, wishing he could fly away like that.

"Yeah," he said, "but that van don't worry me."

He was good at lying.

"Well, it should. You know what happens when it's on the prowl." Pete coughed, hard and racking, phlegm catching in his throat.

Kid turned to face Pete. The old fella appeared a brown bundle of rags with a grey mop sitting on top, his cardboard sign saying NO FUTURE never far away. Pete's hair hung in lank strips, the ends

19

well past his shoulders. A straggly beard and moustache hid a mouth that was capable of giving a cheesy grin from time to time. All right, the teeth were chipped and dirty like Mum's, but Kid loved *that* particular smile.

"They won't get me," Kid said, confident he had his wits about him enough to evade capture.

"That's what the others said, and where are they now, eh?" Pete drew one arm from the many folds of fabric around him and stood from his crouch. He took an ancient-looking metal pole in hand and poked inside the oil drum. Orange sparks flew up, the cold air extinguishing them to nothing. "We don't know where they are because they were taken somewhere, weren't they. One minute they're round and about, and the next, the van comes and them young blokes are gone."

"Maybe they moved on elsewhere." But Kid didn't believe that.

"Maybe they did," Pete said. "But you and I know the truth. Like I told you, that van comes every six months. I see it out there on the streets. Like a big monster, it is, smooching the damn kerb, all slow, like. Whoever's inside it, well, they're not right. They're up to something."

Kid pushed off the bridge and walked towards the fire. He held his hands out over the heat, grateful his fingers were thawing. He ought to get some gloves, and his shoes needed replacing. His had splits in the soles. It wasn't so bad if it didn't rain, but getting small stones inside them was a right bitch.

20

"If I stay with you I'll be safe, so the van isn't a problem for me." Kid rubbed his hands.

"Yeah, well, you know how it goes. Some nights we sleep in different places. There'll be a time that van'll come for you." Pete leant the pole against the wall. He resumed his former position, knees clicking as he lowered to the ground.

Kid's stomach contracted, and he swallowed bile. "I'm not scared."

"Oh, you're scared all right. You just don't show it."

"Nah, I'm not scared."

Kid hunkered down on the other side of the oil drum so Pete couldn't see his face. Dad always said he could tell when he lied because his cheeks went red. Granted, the fire had warmed his skin, but he didn't fancy Pete knowing the real reason his face blazed.

"I reckon you ought to tell me your real name, Kid. Just in case the van comes for you."

"I don't need to tell you because the van isn't coming for me. Told you that already." Kid pulled his arms from his sleeves then hugged himself inside his coat. For warmth, that was all. Warmth. "Besides, if I told you my name, who would give a shit I was gone anyway?"

"Me. And the police, that's who. I've been talking to them about this for years. Told them about the van. Some copper called Langham. He took me seriously, but the others, they're not listening. Reckon I'm mad, crazy, whatever the fuck they call me. But if I had a name I could give them... Yeah, they'd listen then."

21

Would the van come for Kid? He hugged himself tighter and stared across the river to a disused car park. Long, ratty, yellowed grass shielded his view of the asphalt. Streetlights, no longer lit, the bulbs busted out by some lout or other, stood around the edge, charred fingers pointing at the sky.

He shivered.

From the cold.

Two shafts of light split the darkness, filtering through the strands of grass, showing them up for the unkempt mess they were. Kid couldn't make out the vehicle. He stood. Slid his arms back into his sleeves. Walked back to the opening, squinted, and copped sight of the dark silhouette of a van that was blacker than the darkness beyond. It idled, an intimidating hill of unanswered questions. A faint rain fell, the tiny droplets showcased by the headlights, coming down in diagonal lines until a shunting breeze jostled them to dancing.

The van door opened, and the interior light came on, a smudge of brightness. The tinted windscreen only gave him a glimpse of two shadowy forms inside. One—the driver—got out then strode towards the grass, an aura of illumination around him. He stopped, hands in coat pockets, and stared at Kid.

Heart thumping hard, Kid stared back. He wasn't scared. No, he could take care of himself all right. His breaths left him in stuttered gasps, grey clouds puffing out and dissipating the higher they climbed. Okay, so his legs had weakened a bit, but that was because he hadn't eaten anything since this morning. He was hungry, that was all.

The man turned away, going back to the van then getting inside. He closed the door, the interior light winking out, then reversed the way he'd come.

The car park looked better now in complete darkness.

A shuffle sounded behind him, and Kid turned.

Pete gazed out over the river. "It was the van, wasn't it? I'd know them headlights anywhere."

"Yeah, it was the van. Some bloke got out. Probably just a geezer looking for a lost dog or whatever."

"You believe what makes you happy, Kid, but I'm telling you, they've spotted you somewhere. They're checking you out. Your haunts. Reckon you ought to start sleeping elsewhere in future. Places you've never been before."

Pete shuffled back to his spot beside the oil drum.

Kid watched the car park for a long time. He'd be safe here for tonight, wouldn't he? If Pete didn't mind him snuggling up, he'd be all right.

He walked over to Pete then slid down the wall beside him. When the old man fell asleep, he'd lean into him.

The sounds of the river trickling past and the occasional plop of water dripping from the bridge ceiling was something for Kid to focus on for a while. It wasn't long before the memory of that van infiltrated his mind, though, and he rolled

Pete's words around in his mind, weighing up his options.

"Pete?"

"Yeah, Kid?"

"My name's Isaac. Isaac Croft."

CHAPTER FOUR

Morning. Bollocks.
Langham stood beside a half-dug grave, the red cup of his Thermos in hand, the flask wedged between his feet. Coffee steam warmed his nose and cheeks. Working outside in this kind of weather was a bitch, what with the nip in the air harsh enough to freeze his fingers. The weather in

London couldn't seem to make up its mind. This cold snap was an interloper to the season. It wasn't so bad while he was doing the actual digging. The cab of the great yellow machine parked at the head of the grave at least provided a little warmth, despite the heater being a bit fucked and only working when it had half a mind.

He took another sip, sighed, and stared at the sky. The clouds seemed too heavy to stay up there, like they'd fall if they filled with any more rain. It didn't look like it'd be long before the damn things burst, drenching the ground and possibly mucking up all his hard work—an hour so far gouging a rectangle out of the earth, ready to hold a body and casket in a day or two.

Flicking his cup free of coffee droplets then screwing it back on the flask, he shook his head. His break was over—"Only fifteen minutes, and make sure you don't go a minute over," Reginald kept saying—and he needed to dig down a few more inches before this grave was done.

Scowling, Langham climbed into the digger and stuffed the flask into his backpack. Not long now until lunch, and today he had a tuna baguette. His mouth watered at the thought, and he shut the image of food from his mind. No sense in thinking about what he couldn't eat yet. Reginald would undoubtedly know he'd scoffed it before his actual lunch break. The bloke had a habit of knowing shit like that.

Langham went about finishing the grave on autopilot, his mind going back to Mark. It wasn't good to always have to peer over your shoulder, but what else could the bloke do? Unless he changed jobs or moved away, he'd always run the risk of that strange man coming back to find him. And if Langham cracked this case, as was his intention, Mark might well fare better fucking off out of London anyway. The gang taking the homeless men off the streets might think he'd grassed them up after all. Also, had it been a good idea that Mark had carried on being a gravedigger? If those men were on the lookout for him, it'd stand to reason they'd eventually get hold of him and ask if he'd opened his mouth to the police.

Fuck all I can do about that. If they come for him, they come. This place is watched by police anyway, so if Mark finds himself in trouble, he'll be safe.

He reversed the digger away from the now-finished rectangle then drove it onto a pathway that separated two expanses of grave-dotted grass. Reginald would be along shortly to make sure Langham had finished in the allotted time he'd given him.

Langham drove the digger up the path then over the mounded edge of grass to his left. He had another grave to dig. He headed towards plot five hundred and nine and, cursing the weather, parked then jumped out of the cab, pulled a ball of string and a tape measure from his pocket. The grave was an adult one, longer than the average, and he marked the size by tying the string to small wooden stakes at each corner. Back in the cab, he started the engine and dug yet another last resting place for some poor bastard who currently

27

occupied a space at the funeral home, the probing inspection from the pathologist long finished, *life* long finished.

Tell me why I agreed to this job again?

Rain splatted on the windscreen in fat, intermittent plops, and he turned on the wipers at slow speed. The sky darkened, one minute light, the next a dark grey that promised the rain would soon be a deluge. He could keep working for now—the rain would help soften the earth—but he'd rather be at home or at the station in the warm. Cold weather snaps were one thing, but adding rain to it just got him miserable and downright pissed off.

Langham switched the wipers to high speed— the deluge he'd predicted came crashing down. Christ, the water oozed over the windscreen in one solid sheet, the wipers fighting to make their curved triangular peepholes. Unable to see to work, he switched the engine off to wait it out. The weatherman had forecast rain, and although he hadn't quite got it right—*"A light smattering of precipitation mid-morning, folks, then sunny skies all the way!"*—Reginald could hardly expect him to keep working when he couldn't see what he was bloody doing.

Eating that tuna baguette tempted him. But if he couldn't see through the window, he couldn't watch for Reginald if he happened to come by ready to catch him. He leant down to the footwell to fumble around inside his rucksack, skating his fingers over the clear wrap covering his lunch. It rustled. Lured him to rip it off. Instead, he grabbed his flask and poured some coffee, telling himself if Reginald had a problem with that, then he could go and fuck himself. The cab had already grown cold without the shitty heater on, and Langham needed to keep warm.

He sipped. If only Oliver could get a bloody message or two from spirit, it might mean Langham could kiss this undercover bullshit goodbye.

A shadow flitted past the windscreen. He necked his coffee then quickly screwed the cup back on his flask. Despite telling himself Reginald could go and fuck himself, Langham didn't fancy an argument over him drinking coffee when he'd already had his break. He jammed the flask in his backpack then sat upright to find the shadow flicking back the other way, towards the cab door on his right. Bracing himself for Reginald to fling it wide, expecting to catch him at some misdemeanour, Langham held his breath.

A figure drew close to the side window, indistinct through the slanting sheets of rain. Reginald? He was sure Reginald had on a bright-blue coat earlier, though, so why didn't the bloke have it on now? Maybe he'd put one of the cemetery-issue wax jackets on over the top when the rain had started. Maybe he'd been listening to the radio in their 'staffroom', a small, ancient grey-bricked building on the other side of the graveyard, and had heard the weather wasn't going to let up and turn into sunny skies all the damn way. If it kept up like this, there was nothing much either of them could do until it stopped.

The figure came closer, and the cab swayed with the person hoisting themselves up onto the outside step, pressing their nose to the pane, the end of it a circle, rain lashing around it. The door handle rattled, and the figure drew their face back and opened the door.

It wasn't Reginald standing there on the step.

A man, wax jacket and trousers covering his large frame, and a waterproof fishing hat on, stared in. Rain splashed off the brim, bouncing onto Langham. Heart thumping hard, it took him a moment to get to grips with the fact that a stranger occupied the step. Was this man visiting a grave, hoping to get in the cab until the downpour eased?

"Um, who are you?" Langham shifted over a little because of the rain coming in and wetting his jeans.

A cold wind whipped inside, swirling around the cab and stealing all the warmth he'd cultivated.

The man continued to stare, his black eyebrows furry slugs. A bushy beard grew around a mouth with fleshy lips, the thick moustache beneath a nose that appeared as though it'd been punched a fair few times.

Shit.

"Look, mate…" Langham wished he'd thought to get his phone out so he could contact Fairbrother. "There isn't room for you in here. If you need to get out of the rain, you can go over there to the—"

"Get out." The man's accent was pure London. He widened his eyes, and the furry slugs arched.

"I can't leave the digger," Langham said.

"Get out. Now." The bloke reached out a leather-gloved hand and gripped Langham's wrist.

"I can't." Langham played the part of gravedigger, fighting the copper instinct inside him. "Honestly, I'll lose my job if I let you get in here." He considered starting the engine and shoving the man off the step, but the digger moved so bloody slowly this fella would catch up with him if that was his intention.

"You won't be needing your job where you're going. Now get out."

Yanked hard, Langham jerked forward, the man's words only just registering. Langham pulled back to reach for his rucksack. His phone was in there. Sliding his finger through the top loop, he lifted the bag just as the man tugged harder.

"All right, all right! I'm getting out."

He let him go, and Langham climbed out, cursing himself for the missed opportunity of kicking him in the chest, given his higher vantage point while sitting in the cab.

Too late now.

Rain smacked into him, needle-like and vicious, and his cheeks stung from the assault. He gripped his backpack tightly—as tight as the hold on his upper arm—and stumbled along by his side towards the far corner of the cemetery. A gate there led into a small housing estate via a long, winding, tree-lined path. They'd vanish among the buildings in no time, and seeing as the sky was so dark and the rain would have kept people inside, Langham had no doubt his entry into the estate would go virtually unseen.

31

But if this man was something to do with the case, Langham would play along.

"Where are we going?" he asked.

"To Cricket's place. Now shut up."

CHAPTER FIVE

Oliver was bored shitless. He hated his job and never thought he'd miss spirit talking to him. Typical that they were silent when he needed information to help Langham out.

Stabbing at the teabag floating in one of the many cuppas he was making, Oliver sighed.

But at least it's a job.

God, he annoyed himself by saying that all the time. He said it to Langham, too, more to assure him that everything was fine, even if it wasn't. Still, they were alive. Safe. That counted for a hell of a lot, didn't it? If they'd been shot when those men had come to find them from the Caribbean, it would have been a different story.

Without warning, a vision suddenly filled Oliver's head.

He was the main character in a scenario he'd never been in before. Fists rained down on him, and the skin split above his eyebrow. Burning pain seared his palm, and something sharp scraped beneath his fingernails. The visual went black, and he struggled to breathe. He opened his mouth to suck in air, and what tasted like earth filled it. Damp. Disgusting. Something heavy fell on top of him. Mud? His head was so foggy he couldn't tie it all together.

If this was a message from spirit, it wasn't making much sense.

He shook his head, some of the mud slipping away, lifted a hand—that was a fucking struggle an' all—and reached out. Something heavier than the mud thumped down on his shins, and a spear of pain shot up his legs.

"Fuck! Oh shit!" someone said, frantic and out of breath.

The extra weight lifted, and Oliver gasped in a deep breath, gazing up at a man standing at the edge of what looked like a grave—Oliver's grave.

Langham. The poor bastard appeared scared to death.

Oliver held out an arm for Langham to grasp his hand.

"How did you get down there?" Langham asked.

"Fuck knows. We're being warned of something. That one of us will end up in a grave because of your job."

Langham frowned, knelt, and took Oliver's hand, hauling him into a sitting position.

Oliver put his hand to his eyebrow and winced. "Jesus, that hurts." He blinked. "Anyone else up there?" he whispered, standing.

"Only a hefty bloke in a wax jacket," Langham said. "Got a full beard and drives a black van."

Oliver swallowed. Was he being told about the men who abducted the homeless? He reached up to the lip of the grave. His fingers met with metal, and he pulled it down to lean it against the side. A ladder.

He climbed up three steps and peered out. "Can't see anyone. Where did he go?"

"I don't know, but let's get the fuck out of here. I need to get hold of Fairbrother. Got to tell him the man is something to do with the case."

Oliver climbed the rest of the way out.

"I need to get going," Langham said. "Work out what these bastards are up to."

"You going to be all right?" Oliver asked.

"Um, difficult one, that. See, I'm here with you, but I'm also being taken...somewhere. Let Fairbrother know. And keep under the radar. Don't want you getting into any shit because of me."

Oliver came out of the vision with a jolt. Pulled his phone from his pocket and texted Fairbrother, giving him as much detail as he could remember. Then he rang Langham. His mobile went to answerphone.

"Shit."

Fairbrother texted back: *Stay put. Continue your workday as normal.*

That would be easier said than done if Langham really had been taken by some bloke in a wax jacket. How the fuck was Oliver meant to concentrate for the rest of the day now? He closed his eyes, asking spirit for more information.

They were stubbornly silent.

Another text came back from Fairbrother: *Things are happening here, can't explain, no time, but whatever you do, just do as you're told.*

What the hell was that supposed to mean?

"Bloody thirsty," someone singsonged from the office.

Oliver sighed. If they were that thirsty they could make the drinks themselves. He carried on making the tea to calm himself, placed the cups on a tray, and carried it from small kitchen off the main office. He walked around to each desk, depositing drinks. No one thanked him, most never acknowledged he was even there, and not for the first time he considered either pouring the hot liquid over everyone's heads or walking out.

Neither was an option.

Back in the kitchen, he filled the kettle again to make his own drink. His mind wandered back to the information dump he'd been given. What if something horrible was happening to Langham?

Oliver shuddered. He'd spend his tea break in here, away from those arseholes in the office who treated him like a skivvy. If he went out there, they'd know something was bothering him, and he didn't feel like explaining what he'd seen in his head.

He tried to project thoughts to Langham, wishing he could hear what he was saying like some other people had been able to. His words hit a brick wall, bouncing back at him with laughter tagging along for the ride.

"Oliver!" Martha shouted from the office. "Mr King wants you to post some letters."

Fuck off and leave me alone, Martha. "Be with him in a minute. I'm on my break, the same as you."

"Uh, now, Oliver. Five minutes ago, like."

He had nothing against her accent, but the tone of Martha's voice got right on his nerves. He poured the remainder of his drink down the plughole, swilled out the cup, and left the kitchen, walking towards Eamon King's office.

"Um, Oliver." Martha tapped her long red fingernails on her desk. "Mr King said the letters are in reception."

Reception? Unusual.

Via the double glass doors, he walked out of an office now abuzz with keyboards tapping and phones ringing. The reception area, all thick carpet and walls adorned with photographs that had appeared in previous newspaper editions, held a massive semi-circular desk. Miss Prissy Pants Extraordinaire sat behind it. She acted as though her shit didn't stink, and she was a rung above Martha on the ladder of people Oliver wished he didn't have to work with.

Sighing, he took the pile of letters off the desk then headed for the lift. He jabbed the DOWN button, the number arrows lighting red on the ascent.

"What have you got there?" Prissy asked.

He turned to face her. "Letters Eamon wanted posting."

"Oh, right. I wondered who'd put them there. He must have come in while I was in the ladies'."

The lift dinged. He smiled tightly and stepped inside, pressing the button for the ground floor. He nosed through the post. What was so important that it couldn't wait until later when the postman collected the letters just after four o'clock? Seeing nothing out of the ordinary—each letter addressed with the usual sticky white label—he shrugged.

The lift stopped. The doors slid open. He stepped out into the building's main foyer, black leather sofas and chairs dotted about. Newspapers and magazines stood in rigid piles on low, glass-topped coffee tables. And Selena, the nicest person in the whole building, smiled at him from behind her vast marble-effect desk.

"Off on an errand?" she asked.

"As ever," he said and pushed open one of the steel-edged glass front doors.

A nip bit the air, and judging by the wet ground, it'd been raining hard. The clouds looked like they held shitloads more. *Fucking great.* Not only was he going to get cold, he'd probably get soaked, seeing as the postbox stood two streets away. He'd never make it there and back in time, going by the fast-darkening sky.

He walked on, turned into Fountain Street and spied the red postbox, sitting on the corner where this road formed a T-junction with the one at the top. No one else occupied the street, unless he counted the people living in the houses on either side. Cars had been parked in a haphazard line right down the road. He stared at a van behind the postbox, on the kerb of the road that formed the top of the T. If that driver wasn't careful, some joyriding little twat would shunt him up the rear and do a right bit of damage.

A black van. Fuck…

To add to his panic, oddly, there wasn't much traffic going to and fro up there. Surprising, because there usually was. Oliver drew closer to the postbox. He glanced at the sky. The first splats of new rainfall came down, large droplets few and far between. He recognised them as the prelude to one motherfucking torrent and upped his pace.

At the postbox, he lifted his hand to drop the letters through the slot then turned away to raise the collar of his shirt around his ears. He didn't fancy a wet neck as well as everything else. Facing the way he'd come, he contemplated jogging to work. The raindrops came faster, and he braced himself to run.

Someone grabbed the back of his top.

Oliver spun round, fist raised, ready to give the bastard what for.

A man grinned, blocked Oliver's fist, teeth flashing. "Hello—Oliver, isn't it? Robert's mate? You need to come with me."

CHAPTER SIX

Harris 'Cricket' Kingsley had time to kill before he...killed.

The thought of that gravedigger and his weird friend shitting themselves almost had him laughing. Cricket had slept in, so his men would have picked those two up by now.

Beside him on the bed, his lover, Stephen, hunched up by the headboard, wrapping his arms around his knees, hugging them close to his chest.

"Stop holding your legs." Cricket glared at him.

Stephen's amber eyes darted left and right.

Defiant little prick. Beautifully defiant.

Cricket was aware he frightened him, but really... What *was* it with the men of today? What did it take to get a lover who did as he was told without umpteen questions?

Stephen took in a deep breath and let go of his knees, stretching his legs out. His pretty face showed signs of crying throughout the night. He'd been homeless, standing on the street corner, with no one to notice him being gone. At least that's what Cricket told himself. Stephen had protested when Cricket's men had grabbed him, bundling the skinny wretch into the back of the van. Said he'd only popped out to get some milk for his mother, so what did they want with him?

They all said shit like that.

Stephen had stared at Cricket beside him on one of the bench seats in the van, the vehicle speeding away to Cricket's home.

"What do you want?" Stephen had asked.

"You'll see." Cricket had smiled. "How old are you?"

"Eighteen."

"Perfect."

Now, Cricket itched to reach out and touch him, but he held back. To be with someone so young was thrilling. He could sit there all day and study him. "You know if you don't do what I want I'll kill you, don't you?"

Stephen cleared his throat. Nodded.

"Glad you've accepted that."

Cricket thought about the coming evening. He could have had the gravedigger and his mate killed without his man, Denzell, bringing them to his house. But...no, that wouldn't have been pleasurable. Shit, they deserved a bit of discomfort. He needed to know what they knew, the gravedigger especially. After all, he'd seen Cricket's face at the cemetery when he'd stared through the iron railings.

That had pissed him off.

And now look where they all were.

It had taken a while to find the digger's friend, but Cricket was a patient man.

That patience had paid off.

"I don't need you at the moment," Cricket said, suddenly weary of Stephen.

Stephen sighed. Probably with relief.

Cricket threw thoughts of everything from his head. Then he dozed.

Tiring work, abducting people.

CHAPTER SEVEN

Stephen listened to the sound of Cricket's breaths as they lengthened. Each exhalation cooled his shoulder, and he shuddered, sick of this place already. Sick of Cricket. What the *fuck* had happened? Since when did going out to get milk for his mum turn into *this?*

Tears pricked his eyes. Yeah, he may well be eighteen, a man, but he sure as shit felt younger. Out of his depth.

His mum would be worrying. He never went anywhere without reassuring her as to whether he'd be late and when he'd be back. She fretted. Always had.

'I'm not asking where you're going just to be nosy, but because something might happen to you. At least then I can give the police some idea of your last known whereabouts.'

Had she sensed this coming? Had she? Did she have some premonition that a sick bastard and his cronies would take him off the street and bundle him into a van, the cardboard milk carton squashed underfoot, white fluid bleeding onto the path?

Jesus.

She would have called the police. She would have kept on at them until they listened. That despite him being an adult, him not coming home just wasn't *like* him.

She'd be crying. Wouldn't have slept.

Just like him.

Stephen's eyes itched. How long could he keep sleep at bay, though? How long before exhaustion took hold and didn't let go?

Nausea had him retching. As did Cricket's clammy arm across his belly.

Easing away slowly, Stephen managed to make it to the other side of the bed without waking him. Quietly, he padded towards the en suite, his arsehole sore from the previous night. A fresh round of tears warmed his eyes.

He hadn't cried like this since he was a kid.

In the bathroom, he reached inside an opaque-glass shower stall and set the water to hot. He climbed in. The water scorched him, but he needed the heat to erase Cricket from his skin. He didn't think he'd *ever* get his touch off him.

When will he get bored of me? When?

This was only the second day. Was it only yesterday teatime he'd been taken?

Stephen sat in the mercifully cool tray and used a whole bottle of shower gel, continually cleaning then washing the tainted suds away. The lather disappeared down the plughole, and he wished his emotions could vanish as easily. Steam filled the stall, the tangy, pleasant scent of the shower gel heady and strong.

Yet he could still smell Cricket.

His mind wandered.

His phone. Cricket had taken it away. Said he'd burn the damn thing so the police wouldn't be able to track it. Stephen imagined his mum ringing it every five minutes. Imagined her crushed expression as it clicked to voicemail.

He hated Cricket for what he'd put her through.

Then the thought came that she wouldn't have the milk for her beloved cups of tea. That his little brother, Todd, wouldn't have had any for his cereal. There was no one else to go out and buy it for them. Dad, well, he'd left them years ago, and they didn't mix much with the neighbours. Mum wouldn't want to leave the house in case she missed Stephen when he came back. Todd was too young to go out alone, and besides, even if he *was* older, Mum wouldn't let him out now.

What will they do without me?

The milk's on the path, Mum. They smashed it up. I'm so sorry.

Tears spilled, as hot as the water. A sob tore from his mouth.

The sound echoed.

What had happened after Cricket had slipped a black muslin sack over his head in the van? He couldn't quite remember. So far, his memories had been disjointed, coming back out of sync, the previous not bearing any relation to the next.

He concentrated to recall them in order.

They gave me something. Drugs. Something.

A drink. They'd taken him from the vehicle after a long journey. His legs had gone to sleep, pins and needles, and it was painful to walk. He'd been steered across what felt like grass. Something springy anyway. It had been cold, a feisty breeze blowing through his T-shirt. What had been underfoot had changed to a harder surface. Concrete maybe. The air had become warmer. Smelt of furniture polish and bleach. He'd stumbled down what had sounded like wooden steps. Someone had pressed his shoulders, and he'd sat on a hard chair, the back of it reminding him of one from his school days. Rope had bound his wrists behind the chair, his ankles to the legs.

Fear. He'd never felt it so clearly in his life.

The sack had come off. A blinding light, pointed right at him, had meant seeing was impossible. All he'd been able to make out was that circle of light surrounded by blackness. A blackness so deep and frightening he'd cried for a long time.

I wanted you then, Mum. Called out for you.

He'd been left alone for what seemed like hours.

The click of a door opening had come, and footsteps down the stairs.

Cricket had spoken, his voice soft and creepy. A forceful whisper right beside Stephen's ear. "Welcome to your new home." His footsteps had echoed again, and he'd fumbled in Stephen's jeans pocket to remove his wallet.

Stephen still hadn't been able to see anything but the light and the blackness beyond.

"Stephen Brookes. Charming name. Now, I'm going to give you a drink. You must be thirsty, hmm?"

Stephen had drunk what tasted like lemonade. The bubbles had burnt his throat, and he'd coughed. Something had pricked his arm.

His mind had gone misty after a while. Questions had come at him, rapid-fire fast, and he'd nodded, not knowing what he was nodding for. When the scrape of a table being pushed across the room had bitten into his dulled senses, when a pen had been positioned in his hand, when they'd told him to sign his name or they'd kill his mum...

Yeah, he'd given his consent to do what they wanted to him. Nodded so hard his neck had hurt. Shouted that yes, yes, he'd do whatever they fucking well told him, so long as they left his mum and brother alone.

"Good," Cricket had said. "And despite you thinking we're barbarians, we *will* leave them alone, *if* you stick to your promise. No sense in offing them for the sake of it. Leaves a nasty trail. Can't have that."

The shower water cooled. Stephen wished it was hot again. Hotter than it had been. He still felt dirty. Used. He hated himself, his skin, his arse, everything. He wasn't sure, if he got out of this alive, that he'd feel comfortable with himself ever again. Cricket's phantom touches were there when his hands weren't. His scent was there when he wasn't present. Those cool breaths brushed Stephen's shoulder even now, when Cricket slept in the other room.

His voice circled around inside Stephen's head. '*Do you hate this, boy? Do you? Do you hate me?*'

"Yes, God, yes. I hate you more than I thought it was possible to hate someone. More than my dad, and that's saying something."

"Oh good."

Cricket's voice came, muffled by the splashing water and the shower enclosure. "Get out of there."

No. Please, no more.

Stephen looked up, squinting through the steam, which would be gone soon, since the water cooled more by the second. He stood, muscles screaming and eyelids drooping, and pushed open the stall door. It banged against the wall.

"Here. A towel for you." Cricket had dressed in jeans and a black Nike hoody, the red baseball cap perched on his black-haired head. And those shoes, those damn pointy-toed shoes that didn't go with his clothing.

Stephen took the towel—it was useless not to. He didn't fancy being hit like last night. His back was still sore from the punishment. Even when Cricket had just...done what he had, Stephen had pushed his luck by revealing exactly how he felt.

Wrapping the towel around himself, he bit back the need to tell him to fuck off and leave him be. He'd given him what he'd wanted, hadn't he? Wasn't that enough?

"I have something I need to do, Stephen. I have some guests to talk to when they arrive later on. It might take some time. Plus, I have other business to attend to throughout the day. You may go to your own room, to the living room, and to the kitchen. Oh, and you may use the downstairs toilet. Other than those places, you *don't* go anywhere else. Do you understand?"

Cricket stared at him with eyes that gave Stephen the creeps. They were hooded, black like that darkness when he'd first got here, and a livid pink scar marched down his cheek, thick and long. Why was it that all mean people had scars? Why did every bad bloke in films or books have them?

Stephen nodded. "Yes, I understand."

Cricket walked towards the exit. He turned, placing one hand on the oak jamb, the other on the edge of the matching door. He stared at him again. "Oh, and if you think you can just walk out of here... Jonathan keeps guard in the foyer, Kevin at the back. They're both armed. When they're not available to keep guard, others take their place. All the windows are locked and can't be smashed. And even if you *did* manage to get out, there are dogs on the grounds. Big ones. With sharp teeth. Think of your mum and brother, Stephen, hmm?"

Stephen nodded again, steeling himself not to cry in front of this sadistic fucker.

"Good. I won't bother you again until tonight." Cricket strode out.

Stephen sagged against the side of the stall with relief. At least he'd have some measure of comfort for a while. He dried off, scrubbing hard at his skin until it reddened and grew sore.

Cricket's touch was still on it.

Stephen walked into the bedroom, half expecting him to still be there, even though he'd said he'd be elsewhere. The bed had been made, the quilt smooth, the pillows without head dents. Stephen's clothes spilt out of the washing basket, and a fresh set, complete with shop labels, sat in a pile on the chair in the corner. He dressed absently then placed the tags in the small bin beside the bed. The socks were soft on his feet, but the boxer shorts chafed.

Wincing, he resisted going into the other bedrooms. And there were several—ten closed doors along the landing he stood on and ten opposite. People might still be asleep behind them.

He went downstairs. In the foyer, with its harlequin-tiled floor—the space as big as their living room at home—he glanced towards the front door. The man named Jonathan, the one who'd approached him on the street, stood with his legs apart, hands folded over his chest. A fucking mountain of a bloke, one Stephen wouldn't tackle if he was paid to do it. Near-white eyebrows rested in a straight line above eyes so blue Stephen wondered if the man had coloured contacts.

Jonathan lifted his chin by way of greeting. Stephen lowered his eyes and headed towards the kitchen. He was hungry, had been since he'd left home, what with popping to the shop just before Mum had dished the dinner up. But could he eat now? He hadn't managed to last night.

In the kitchen, he glanced around, still surprised at the opulence even though he'd seen this room already. Fuck, how much did Cricket earn? And what did he *do* for a living? The house was massive, and everything in it must have cost a pretty penny.

Stephen went over to the double-wide fridge. He pulled open both doors. It was filled with everything a person could want, a vast difference from theirs at home, which held what they needed for each week and nothing more. He peeked in the freezer. Packed to fucking bursting.

He had the taste for pizza despite the morning hour. A Domino's box rested on a shelf. He lifted the lid. Meat feast.

While waiting for it to heat in the microwave, he browsed the room, taking in the stark white cupboards and the black tiled floor. Everything was so neat and tidy. So clean. Nothing homely about it, all pristine and perfect like some show house. He puffed out a laugh.

Mum was right. If you're rich, you can have anything. Do anything. Including abducting people and fucking their arse whenever you bloody well please.

The microwave dinged. He took his plate out and settled gingerly on a café stool at the breakfast bar that spanned the end of the room farthest from the door. He glanced to his left, through the black slatted blinds. Nothing out there but a great expanse of grass and a small forest at the bottom. He shuddered at the thought of people like Jonathan and Kevin standing guard down there in the shadows, guns at the ready.

There were no dogs.

A faint sun struggled to shine in the murky grey-blue. It would be ages before it changed places with the moon. A long day ahead.

He ate a whole slice, then a yell came from behind a door to his right. Why hadn't he noticed that there before? He stared at it—a keyhole beneath the brass handle, but no key. Was that where the 'guests' were?

He took a moment to think, then approached the door and dared to try the handle. He lowered it slowly, but the door didn't budge. Like it would be unlocked. Another yell came and, like the last, it wasn't one of pain but of anger. Someone was frustrated and needed to shout to release some tension.

What was going on?

The shouts had been muffled, as though far away.

Curious, yet scared shitless in case Jonathan or Kevin came in any minute, Stephen went down on his haunches. He peered through the keyhole.

A long corridor, lit by spotlights recessed in the ceiling. Several plain white doors on either side, spaced out as if each room was maybe eleven by eleven. One door at the end, different from the rest, mahogany, studded with carved squares.

Someone shouted again. Angry. Violent.

Another voice came, plaintive, heart-wrenching. "Mum! I want me mum!"

"Oh fuck," Stephen whispered.

They have someone else in there. They abducted someone else?

He went back to his seat. Sat and stared at the cooling pizza, unable to eat another bite. What the hell kind of place had he been brought to? Bile zipped up into his mouth, acidic on his tongue. He swallowed, desperate for a drink of water. He filled a glass. Gulped down the cool liquid, standing stock-still, waiting for it to come back up.

It did, a fluid fountain, splashing up the sides of the white sink.

Frantic, petrified he'd be caught making a mess, he ran the tap to clean up, thankful the pizza had stayed down. Another shout, this time one of pain, chilling Stephen to the bone. What were they *doing* to whoever had cried out like that? *Who* was doing it? Cricket? One of his men?

Shutting out the questions, he cleared his plate, glass, and cutlery away.

Unable to stand being in the kitchen with yet more sounds coming through that door, he rushed out into the foyer. Jonathan's smile freaked him the fuck out, and he ran up the stairs into his room, slamming the door and pressing his back against it.

He'd been brought into a nightmare, one he didn't think he'd ever get out of and, like that person had said earlier, he whispered, "Mum. I want me mum."

CHAPTER EIGHT

Langham winced at the pain biting into the top of his arm. He struggled to break free of the man's hold, but the bastard wouldn't let go. His phone had trilled with a voice message alert, but he'd been unable to answer it.

Had it been Oliver or Fairbrother?

"Who the fuck are you?" Langham asked.

The bearded man gripped tighter. He glanced sideways at Langham, sheeting rain wetting his cheeks. The hairy slugs drew together at the top of his nose, and his lips disappeared inside that thick beard.

Langham shuddered, a few droplets of rain finding their way down his coat collar. The only thing swirling in his mind was the stark fact he was being dragged along an alley.

A large black Transit with tinted windows sat parked on the kerb at the end. It reminded him of the one used by the A-Team. At any other time, and any other situation, he'd have pissed himself laughing.

Christ. Shit!

"What does this Cricket want with me?" he demanded.

"You're Robert Briggs." Beardy stared at him again and dug his fingers in harder.

"Yeah. So?" Langham clamped his jaw and glared, jogging to keep up with his fast walk.

"Then you're the man I'm after. Now shut the *fuck up*, all right?"

They reached the end of the alley. Beardy glanced left then right. Langham did the same. The street was empty of people. Typical. What he wouldn't give for someone to come out of their house now, on their way to getting the shopping. Or for someone to be cleaning their windows. Mind you, this wasn't the kind of estate where anyone cleaned their windows, and if Langham was seen being bundled into a van by a fuck-off

58

burly bloke, the residents would more than likely keep their mouths shut.

Criminals looked after their own.

"Come on." The man tugged him to the van.

Beardy flung the back doors open then shoved Langham forward. Refusing to get in, Langham tried grip the road with his boots, but the bloody things wouldn't hold on to the wet surface. Pushed in the back, he went sprawling forward, the edge of the van floor jabbing just below his knees. His hands slapped onto a square of rough blue carpet, the fibres chafing his palms.

"Look, I'm not going with you until you tell me what—"

Hauled up by the back of his jacket and unceremoniously dumped inside, he cracked his temple on one of the two metal bench seats down either side and curled himself into a ball. If he played scared, he might fare better. Hand over the injury, he scrunched his eyes closed and focused his mind away from the spearing pain. "Jesus *Christ!*"

Beardy climbed in and bent at the waist, fists bunched and ready. The scent of rain came off him. He shoved Langham onto his back and planted a heavy boot on his stomach. "Now, do as you're fucking told, or things will get worse for you, yeah? Cricket wants you brought back. Wants some questions answered. I'm just the collection boy, know what I'm saying? Like, don't shoot the messenger. Get up." He took his foot away and straightened, staring down at him.

Langham got up onto his knees, head throbbing, and pushed the bench top with his hands to help him stand. Out of breath from the anger that surged through him, he glared at the man, his heart thumping hard, his jaw muscles aching from clenching his teeth. "I don't know anything. All I do is dig graves."

He had to make it look authentic that he was just some random bloke and not a copper. But meeting this Cricket? Yeah, that would do nicely.

"Oh, you're going to a worse place now, mate, and believe me, the surroundings might be nicer, but the torture is something else. Sit." Beardy reached into his jacket, producing a bright-yellow cable tie.

Oh fuck.

"Drop your bag and hold your wrists out."

Langham obeyed, eyeing the way to freedom behind his abductor, quickly working out whether, if he nutted him in the guts, he'd make it out and back to the cemetery in time to use his phone or get help.

As though it had been planned this way, still no one occupied the street.

"Don't bother." Beardy secured Langham's wrists. "No one will come out to help you. Quiet here this time of day. People at work and whatnot." He slid the end of the tie through the small square that would keep him bound. "And no cars driving about. Funny that, eh?"

"Who the hell *are* you?" Langham drew in a sharp breath—the cable tightened and dug into his skin. He knew how to break them, but he wouldn't do so until he'd gleaned more information.

"I'm friends with people who have a lot of clout." He took hold of Langham's backpack handle. "You won't be needing this."

Fuck, my phone...

The bully poked about inside. "Baguette. Aren't you thoughtful. I didn't have breakfast this morning. This'll do go down a treat, thanks."

He climbed out, Langham's backpack bumping the side of his leg. The doors slammed, leaving him trying to work out how he could get word to Fairbrother. Or even Oliver. Maybe he ought to try that mind-joining thing again, where he thought stuff and Oliver heard it.

"Fuck it!" he whispered.

He lifted his bound hands and cradled his forehead. Rain bounced on the roof, exacerbating the throb in his temples.

Beardy got in then drove away. Langham watched through the window, making a mental note of the streets they drove down. The van came to a stop at the top end of Fountain Street.

Beardy climbed out.

"Oi!" Langham shouted, glancing towards the driver's seat.

A metal grate with a small door in the centre partitioned him off from the front of the van. What was this, a former prison vehicle? He caught sight of an old man in the passenger seat, his head facing forward. Beardy paced back and forth past the windscreen, phone clamped to his ear. The rain drenched him despite his hat and coat.

"Don't bother wasting your time," the old man said. "He's a nasty one."

Langham leant forward and narrowed his eyes.

"I'm Eamon King," the fella said. "Oliver's new boss." He turned his head a little to look through the grate, seeming to want to keep his other eye on the man outside. "He's here to collect Oliver next. Heard him there, talking on the phone." He nodded to the windscreen.

Langham frowned, battling to comprehend the madness of this situation. "How did you...? What did he...?"

"Got hold of me this morning. Early. At the printing warehouse after I'd nipped into the office."

"But it's around about eleven o'clock now. What's he been doing with you since then?" Langham's mind went crazy, questions popping up too fast for him to answer them.

"They saw Oliver drop you off at work yesterday—bit stupid, if you don't mind me saying so. You undercover and whatever—Oliver told me that, by the way. Oliver had to go to the printing warehouse for me yesterday. They followed him. Thought that was where he worked. When they turned up there this morning and Oliver wasn't there, they nabbed me instead." He turned fully to Langham and pointed to his face.

A bruise was coming out just below Eamon's left eye.

"Jesus." Langham swallowed.

These men meant business. But then he'd known they were bad through and through. Had to be if they were snatching people off the bloody street.

The future didn't look too bright.

Langham cleared his throat. "So where have you been since they met up with you this morning?"

"Driving around. They made me tell them things. Threatened me. Got me to tell them that Oliver worked in my office. Then that bloke with the beard there got hold of some other one on the phone, a man called Fairbrother or something, and ranted about needing a street cleared. Something about roadblocks."

What? "Fairbrother. Did you say *Fairbrother?*"

"Yeah."

Shit. If it's the same one, is Fairbrother a dodgy copper?

"Did he say whether he was letting you go?" Langham jerked his head towards the bearded man, who was still speaking into the phone as though angry, cheeks stained pink.

"Yes. If I do what they want and keep my mouth shut after." Eamon gave a wry chuckle. "And if this debacle is anything to go by, I'm doing as I'm told. Besides, the threat to my family— He's coming. Shh."

Beardy swiped his phone then climbed into the van. "Right, now we wait."

"What d'you want this old fella for?" Langham asked.

"Keep your fucking nose out," Beardy said, his tone weary.

"Just do as he says." Eamon kept his gaze forward.

Beardy's arm shot out, his fist connecting with the editor's cheek. "And you can keep your nose out an' all."

Eamon's head smacked into the side window, and he let out a whimper. The poor bastard hadn't deserved that.

"Leave it out, will you?" Langham looked at Beardy in the rearview mirror.

Beardy sighed. "Shut. The fuck. Up." He paused, then, "Or the old man gets another one."

Langham clamped his lips together and breathed heavily through his nose. Adrenaline surged through him. Who the hell hit old men?

Evidently, people who worked for a bloke named Cricket.

It was on the tip of his tongue to ask who Cricket was again, to see if Fairbrother was the same one he knew, to find out more information, but he stopped himself.

The rain had ceased a bit, but it looked like it wouldn't be long before it pelted full force again. Langham had the inane thought that the weatherman needed shooting for giving out the wrong information.

Beardy swivelled in his seat so he faced Eamon. "Right, I'm just waiting on someone else doing their part of the job, then we'll be on our way."

Langham bowed his head, staring at the carpet. Easing forward, he pinched some of the fibres and, although it was awkward, managed to put them in his jacket pocket. Who knew whether they'd come in handy later for Fairbrother? *If* Langham was lucky enough to get out of this shit and he could hand them over. *If* Fairbrother wasn't dodgy. But if he wasn't? Well, there'd be evidence, wouldn't there.

He closed his eyes while Eamon blathered on about obeying every order he was given, the poor old duffer's voice quivering and full of fear. The sound of a sigh of impatience got Langham's head snapping up, and he peered through the grate. The old man shook as though a palsy victim.

He'll fucking have a heart attack in a minute.

"Once Oliver's in the back, you can go," Beardy said to the editor.

They're getting Oliver, too? Shit. Fuck.

Beardy stared at Eamon. "No need to tell you he won't be returning to work in the morning. Reckon you'll be busy this afternoon putting a job ad in the paper."

Langham's guts churned.

Beardy stared past Eamon and down the street to their left. "Won't be long and you can get back to your newspaper, me old mate." He rasped a hand over his beard. "Now, both of you be quiet. I'm getting a fucking headache."

Langham peered down Fountain Street, straining his eyes for the first sight of Oliver. He spotted another black van parking by the postbox. Was he in there?

Oliver was roughly manhandled out of the van. Langham thought of lunging forward, hammering his fists on the rear windows, but what good would that do?

65

In his peripheral vision, he caught sight of Beardy's fist shooting towards Eamon again.

Shit.

The editor's sobs added to the weight of guilt pouring down on Langham's shoulders. He reared back and slumped onto the bench seat, a huge breath gushing out of him. Dejection took hold, sheer helplessness that he was a grown man and couldn't do a bloody thing to stop this madness.

Oliver was brought closer by a tall, wide man. Langham resisted the need to leap forward again. Beardy had eased open the driver's-side door, one hand on the steering wheel.

The rain pelted down.

Beardy left the van. Langham glanced at Eamon, who sat with his head bent, shoulders bobbing. Turning away and looking back at Oliver, Langham sucked in a breath.

Oliver! Shake him off. Fucking run!

Beardy approached them and grabbed Oliver's jacket. Oliver swung around, fist raised. His eyes widened along with his mouth. Beardy yanked him towards the van, and Oliver tried to stop him, digging his feet into the ground.

It won't work.

Beardy and Oliver walked to the back of this van. Langham scooted along the bench, ready to kick out at Beardy the minute the door opened. His breaths stuttered, and pains lanced his chest, his heart rate picking up speed.

"Please don't do anything stupid," Eamon whimpered. "He'll take it out on my family."

Beardy pre-empted Langham and kept Oliver in front of him. Oliver's face pressed against a door window, and Beardy fumbled inside his jacket. Cable tie. Beardy yanked Oliver's arms behind him and worked on his wrists, and Oliver jolted against the glass, his cheek white from the pressure.

We're fucked. So fucked if spirit doesn't talk to him. If we can't get out of these ties and let Fairbrother know what's going on. Or Sergeant Villier—she'd be a better bet now if Fairbrother's bent.

Beardy shoved Oliver aside, meaty hand gripping his upper arm. He opened a door. Oliver spotted Langham, and his mouth worked with no sound coming out. Face paling, he blinked then frowned. Beardy sent him lurching onto the van floor. He closed the door quickly behind him just as Langham flung out a foot. The end of his boot smacked into the door, and he bit back a yell, his toes mashing into the steel toecap inside. He pushed Oliver onto his side. Oliver's eyes were closed, and a nasty gash on his forehead bled, a crimson river dribbling down his temple.

"Fuck! Wake up, mate. Wake up!"

Langham went down on his knees, barely aware of Beardy getting back into the van and telling Eamon to get out. Breaths unsteady, his heart beating way too fast, Langham leant forward, cheek above Oliver's nose.

He was still breathing.

Langham hauled him into a sitting position. He dragged him to the space behind the passenger seat so he could watch Beardy while tending to

Oliver. He sat wedged in the corner, hefting his friend against him, and stared through one of the rear windows. Eamon ran down the street, his bandy legs looking like they'd give out any second.

Langham turned back to Oliver.

"I'll fucking have you for this," he snarled at Beardy.

Beardy started the engine then nosed away from the kerb. "Whatever, mate. Whatever."

CHAPTER NINE

Oliver's mouth seemed full of cotton wool. His clock radio blared, some song where the singer was young, free, and all right. *Lucky him.* He kept his eyes closed, recalling the fuck-off weird dream he'd just had where he'd been at work and sent out to post letters. That was off in itself. Eamon had said he was a stickler for routine and the post must never be collected before four p.m. Some bloke had grabbed Oliver at the postbox and put him inside a black van, leaving him there for a while. Then he'd been led to yet another van down the road. Had his wrists tied. Langham had been inside, his wrists tied, too, and Oliver had smacked his head on the van floor and blacked out.

So bloody strange.

He moved his head—was it leaning on Langham's arm?—and tried to prise his heavy eyelids open. They refused to budge. One seemed stuck closed with sleepy dust. He frowned, the world around him trying to penetrate the fug of sleep.

Was that the sound of an engine? And was the bed *rocking?*

Realisation slammed into him at the shriek of brakes and the other side of his body lurching into something hard. He snapped his eyes open, flung back the other way, staring at the bench opposite. Fuck. He hadn't been dreaming.

Shit!

Turning his head, grimacing at the pain in his forehead and at his bound wrists behind him, he glanced at Langham, whose head had flopped back into the corner. He slept, and Oliver would bet if Langham knew he'd dropped off, he'd be pissed off. Oliver looked through a metal grate between the back of the van and the front. The bloke who'd shoved him in here tapped the steering wheel, clearly agitated he'd had to stop at a red light.

Oliver's heart rate sped up, and a ball of something lodged in his chest.

Fear? Anxiety?

Both, probably.

How long had they been travelling? He'd posted the letters around eleven this morning, and it was clearly evening now. Dark-grey clouds scudded across a navy-blue sky speckled with faint stars. What looked like shops—what he could see of them anyway, the rooms above them, perhaps— lined either side of the road. Lights blazed from some of the windows, and a green-and-pink neon sign in the shape of a scantily clad woman flashed on and off high up on a building wall. A club?

Fresh raindrops clung to the outside edges of the windscreen, indicating a recent downpour, but the wipers weren't swishing to and fro. Light made the droplets appear as diamonds, shimmering and perfect on a van holding an imperfect driver and abducted passengers.

Oliver craned his neck in order to get a better view, to see below the shop signs. See *people*. Not many walked the street, but there were enough to show him it was well into the evening, their clothes making it clear they were out for a night on the town. Women in short skirts and halter-neck tops. Men in jeans, dress shirts untucked, hands in suit jacket pockets. Smart casual. This wasn't some dowdy area then, it was more upmarket than most places.

He studied the scenery for a street sign, anything to give him some clue.

Where the fuck are we?

He didn't need to ask the why—this had something to do with Langham being undercover, didn't it? Yeah, he'd been waiting for this to happen, but hadn't *really* thought it would.

Why *was* that? The gang had been organised in abducting men. They meant business.

The lights turned green. The big bearded bastard pulled off smoothly and blended into traffic in the next lane. Horns honked, loud and persistent, drivers protesting that the man in control of this van should have been in the correct lane in the first place. That the bloke had to veer across like that screamed his mind was occupied with other things. Maybe if Oliver scooted down to the doors and tried to open them, they could get out, van moving or not, and find help.

Like he's going to have left them unlocked.

He and Langham weren't going anywhere except the driver's destination. Unless Fairbrother had backup following them. Maybe once they arrived there'd be an opportunity to get the fuck away.

He jerked his shoulder, the one pressing on Langham, gently trying to wake him. The volume of the radio, blasting about some woman who kept bleeding love, would disguise anything they had to say. They could make a plan.

Or something.

Yeah, running with my hands tied behind my back will be a fucking breeze.

"Langham!" he said, voice low.

Langham snapped his eyes open. Glanced from the driver to Oliver. He let out a sigh and briefly closed his eyes again. "You all right? Shit, I fell asleep."

"Yeah. I'm fine. Head hurts, but I'm okay." Oliver shot a look at the driver then propped his chin on Langham's shoulder so he could speak with less chance of being overheard. "I had the thought of trying the door, but as we know, these men are from a fucking big outfit. Don't make mistakes often, know what I mean?"

Langham nodded, eyes narrowed.

"So," Oliver said, "when we get to wherever it is we're going, d'you reckon we can make a run for it?"

"Depends where we're heading. Although I don't want you involved, we might be better off going inside wherever we end up. Bound to be phones. And I can get more information."

"How did he get hold of you? What happened?"

Langham explained. Oliver listened, anger boiling inside him. These fucking tossers were something else, weren't they. Who the hell did they think they were? And as for them snatching Eamon...shit, he was surprised the old duffer hadn't died of shock. His boss being hit didn't sit well. No need for that kind of thing, was there. An old bloke posed no threat whatsoever, even if he *was* irritating. The driver was just being an arsehole. Showing who was in charge. Oliver would like to see how in control the man was with a boot in his bollocks. No matter how strong a fella was, their crown jewels being whacked always bent them double—unless they had steel jockstraps on.

He presumed the road by the postbox had been blocked off. They had to have some contacts to be able to get that sort of thing done.

Langham had said the boss's name was Cricket, but Oliver had never heard of him.

"If we *are* being taken to him, then..." Oliver scrunched his eyes closed to loosen the tight skin on his cheek.

"Dried blood." Langham nodded towards the wound. "Thank fuck that gash stopped bleeding. Thought for a minute back there it wouldn't."

"Is it bad?" Oliver wanted to touch it. A burst of irritation sparked inside him at being unable to. He stared at Langham's bound wrists and guessed his own sported a gaudy yellow cable tie, too. *Tasty.*

If he didn't crack an internal joke or two, he'd break under the pressure.

"It'll leave a scar. Too late for it to be sewn up." Langham eyed the driver again. "He's a right wanker. No way we're going to be able to get away from him."

"But there's two of us now," Oliver said.

"It depends on how many are at the other end. Who knows where we're going? Who's to say there isn't an army of nutters waiting for us when we arrive?"

A dark thought hit Oliver. "Who's to say we're being taken any place where there *are* people. Might be some warehouse. Torture equipment set up." His imagination ran riot. "A river close by. Ready for us to be dumped into. Drowning. You know what these gangland fellas are like—"

"All right, all right!" Langham said. "I get it." He sighed again, a bloody great big one, and shook his head slowly.

The image of concrete blocks around their ankles entered Oliver's head—Jesus, that was a difficult one to get rid of. It sat in his mind, a sentinel, refusing to budge no matter how hard he tried to conjure another vision. But it wasn't a message from spirit. It was his mind fixing the thought there through his fear.

He sniffed, blinked, cleared his throat. "I'm not going down without a fight."

"Me neither."

They sat in silence for a time, the place they'd driven through giving way to countryside. Trees stood starkly in the beam of the headlights, moss-covered skeletons, skinny hands clawing the blackness. The road was narrow. If another driver approached from the other way, the driver slowed. He veered to the left each time, and branches from hedges scraped the side of the van, sending Oliver's mind reeling with the creepy image of long, dirty fingernails scratching, the dead trying to get in at them. It seemed as if death waited, wearing a disguise as the air in the van, a tangible thing, smothering them, letting them know it would be their turn to die soon.

"I'm sorry my job keeps bringing us crap," Langham said.

"Don't be." Oliver gave him a sidelong glance. "Wouldn't change a fucking thing."

A large green road sign edged in white stood up ahead, taking Oliver's attention from morbid thoughts. The white glowed from the headlights, but he couldn't read the wording yet. From the image on the sign of a road and a roundabout at the top, he hoped they approached civilisation. Well, he did and he didn't. While they travelled, they were relatively safe.

He nudged Langham. "Road sign coming up."

Langham straightened and looked through the windscreen. Oliver had to lean across in order to see, but the words became clear. They were still in London, only a few miles away from where they'd been picked up. *What the hell?* Roads to various other surrounding places sprouted off the roundabout image.

"Has he been driving around London all day or what?" Oliver said.

"Probably. Who fucking knows. We were asleep." Langham leant back against the side of the van and stared at the ceiling. "What does it matter where we're bloody going? The result will be the same whether we're in Camden Town, Ladbroke sodding Grove, or somewhere else."

Fuck.

Had Langham given up? Was this one case too many? Oliver recognised defeat in his eyes, in the slump of his shoulders. Langham might think *this* time it was the end of the road. They had no idea what lay up ahead, but there might be all manner of opportunities presented to them in the near-distant future. Ones where they could try to get away. Spirit might get in contact, because if they didn't...

Those concrete blocks didn't appeal.

Dying in *any* fashion didn't appeal.

The van going around the roundabout had Oliver watching out of the windscreen again. His shoulders ached from his arms being wedged behind him, and craning his neck added to the pain. But if, as he suspected, the pain was going to get worse later on, and meted out by bullies' fists and whatever else they chose to use, he could stand it for now.

Streetlamps around the edge of the roundabout gave the sky a strange, muted orange glow and enhanced the blackness beyond. Oliver shivered involuntarily and held his breath, waiting to see which road the driver took. The big bastard ignored the main London fork prong and continued round then slewed onto a road that led elsewhere. Oliver's stomach rolled over as yet more countryside whipped past.

The concrete blocks were becoming more of a reality than he'd like.

We could still be going to some nearby town or other. Somewhere we can get help.

He chuckled at the unlikelihood of that. These blokes would have a hideout. Obvious, wasn't it?

As though his thoughts had predicted the truth, the van slowed then turned right down a rutted track. Trees, branches bare and knobbly, lined either side, creating a filigree canopy overhead. The headlights picked out the track—tightly packed, dark mud that the rain had barely penetrated. A stripe of grass ran down the middle, brushing the undercarriage as the van trundled on. Ahead, the lights of a building shone out, several yellow squares and a few dots that Oliver supposed were garden lamps.

His pulse throbbed in his neck.

"Shit," he said.

"Fuck." Langham turned his head and stared out. "A bastard house in the middle of sodding nowhere."

Oliver studied it. Massive place, all cream façade and fake Greek columns standing behind a high, black wrought-iron fence. Four Victorian streetlamps, two either side of a cream-coloured gravel drive, stood directly outside the house. Wide stone steps led from the end of the driveway up to the black double front doors.

Mansion. Who said crime doesn't pay?

"Blimey," Oliver muttered, awed by the magnificence despite fear nipping at his arsehole.

The van slowed as it neared the gates, which swung open. Someone had seen them coming then, letting them into the grounds. The vehicle jostled over the uneven gravel, and the driver leant forward to switch off the radio. He did a U-turn then backed up to the house. Got out. Slammed the door.

The back doors opened too soon.

"Out," the driver said. "Now."

CHAPTER TEN

Cricket prowled his vast living room. Denzell had arrived right on time. *There* was a young man he'd saved from a crap life. Denzell had been homeless, living down an alley in Bethnal Green, a sheet of cardboard for a mattress. Cricket had him picked up and brought here so he could be primed for the next stage in his life. He was supposed to have lived as some rich man's arse, getting everything he desired, but Cricket had kept him as an employee. Whether Denzell was happy doing that, Cricket didn't give a shit. He provided what punters ordered, simple as that, and if Denzell didn't like having anything to do with that, tough.

Besides, Cricket was doing society a favour, ridding the streets of potential criminal scumbags. Even those who weren't homeless had the possibility of becoming a bad element, didn't they? That he sold them to the highest bidder was by the by. In the end, everyone was happy. Apart from the parents. And maybe the snatched lads if they didn't like their arses being stretched on a nightly basis.

He chuckled at the naïvety of some parents. They thought they were safe because they had sons, didn't they. Thought only girls went missing. Little did they know, until *their* kid got taken, boys were more in demand.

He laughed and picked imaginary specks from his black suit, then wiggled the knot of his dark-grey tie. His new white shirt had been dry-cleaned, but it still held stiffness in the collar. It dug into his skin. Pissed him off.

Denzell had done well today, executing the plan. The roadblock idea had been a good one, and Denzell had sorted everything himself without bothering him with the details.

A fine man, Denzell. Ugly as fucking sin, but a fine man all the same. Loyal bastard, that one.

He strode to one of the two large bay windows. Stared out across the lawn at the black van and its cargo.

This had been Denzell's first solo outing. He'd had to earn Cricket's trust since starting to work for him a few months back. Not all his employees had taken to this life, and those who hadn't were no longer...a problem.

Twin spots of brightness blared through the window. Headlights. Denzell had proven his loyalty. Cricket admitted he'd been a little worried he wouldn't come back, wouldn't do whatever needed to be done to get hold of those two men and bring them here.

Cricket released a held breath. Straightened his already straight jacket. Smoothed his tie. Rolled his shoulders and blew out another nerve-steadying breath. He always experienced an edgy excitement at times like this. He got to go back to his roots, didn't he, beating the fuck out of someone until they spewed everything they knew. Yeah, he'd started his career as a bully boy and worked his way up. Stuck to his patch and minded his own business, refrained from stepping on other main men's toes. It didn't do to piss off a London crime boss, did it? Cricket's intuitiveness had paid off, and here he was now, a respected crime boss himself, with a fucking big mansion, shitloads of money, and a nice piece of arse to show for it.

He moved to a strip of wall between the windows and pressed a button on the keypad there. The gates at the end of the driveway swung closed. His belly clenched with the anticipation of what was to come. After Cricket had a little chat and a beating session with the captives, he'd be hyped up, manic energy flicking through his body.

Perhaps he'd give Stephen a visit.

Prodding a button on the keypad again, he said into the speaker below, "Prepare them. Let me know when they're ready."

"Okay, boss."

Jonathan was a good man, too.

Cricket stared at the cargo. They stood, heads bowed, the one from the graveyard with his hands bound to the front. Robert Briggs. Oliver Banks' hands were behind his back. The house front doors creaked open, the sound filtering to him.

Jonathan went out and took hold of Briggs' arm, and Denzell took Oliver's. His men propelled the shipment up the steps and into the house. Cricket turned to face the living room door, the one that led out to the foyer, and tuned in to the sounds out there. The snatched men appeared to be doing as they'd undoubtedly been told—keeping bloody quiet. Feet squeaked on the tiled floor, their footsteps receding as they were marched down to the kitchen.

Cricket turned again, his back to the windows, and listened for the door beside the breakfast bar to open then close. Once it had, he spun to his right and faced the wall populated with art. Behind the pictures were ten rooms off a long white corridor, and at the end was the cellar door. A place where all manner of scenes were acted out in the play that was his life. The play he orchestrated. The one his mentor, Parker, had written all those years ago.

Ah, Parker. Our time together was so short...

Cricket paced some more, waiting for the call to tell him the abductees had been prepared for his visit. It came a few minutes later via a crackle from the wall speaker.

"In position, boss."

Without responding to Jonathan, Cricket left the living room and strode through the foyer to the kitchen. He gripped the door handle that led to the corridor and closed his eyes, inhaling a steadying breath.

Footsteps coming from behind the door snapped him out of his trance. He threw the door wide. Jonathan and Denzell walked towards him, coming through into the kitchen.

Cricket nodded and stepped into the brightly lit, white-walled corridor. He closed then locked the door behind him and remained still, staring down at the cellar door, listening for sounds coming from any of the holding rooms. They held the young men waiting to be chosen tomorrow night by prospective buyers. They'd all had their arses tested by Cricket, and he'd found each of them to be worthy of being sold on. A few had needed fattening up—but not too much. His buyers liked them slim.

The customer was always right.

Cricket closed his eyes and breathed deeply upon someone shouting out for his mother.

She's no good to you now.

Opening his eyes, he smiled and strolled down the corridor, pleased at the sound his shoes, with the three hundred pound price tag, created. He'd dreamt of owning such shoes as a boy after seeing another, older gangland boss in them, the pointed toes appealing to his nasty side.

The tips were good for kicking.

He rolled his shoulders, and the collar of his shirt squeaked, chafing his skin. At the end, he stood in front of the mahogany studded door. He smelt those two new bastards and their fear from here.

Key in the lock, he turned it and opened the door. A set of concrete steps, matching walls either side, led down to a square landing. He locked the door. Took the steps slowly, turning right on the landing then going down the remaining stairs and into the dark cellar.

One of the cargo whimpered.

He smiled again.

Cricket reached the wall on his left and flicked a switch. A bright circle of light shone directly on the men—so they couldn't see him in the surrounding darkness. The pair of them hung from chains secured to the metal ceiling rafter, their arms stretched upwards, naked bodies probably already screaming for respite.

Cricket had no intention of killing them now. This morning he'd wanted to, he'd been frantic to kill, but he'd thought better of it since seeing them close up like this. Both were brawny enough to handle themselves in a fight, and Cricket was always in need of men to pick up the homeless. A bit of a beating and the threat of them being offed if they didn't work for him might do the trick.

"All right, wankers?" he asked.

They jolted, and one of them—Cricket couldn't tell which—gasped.

"I realise you might not want to answer me. That's all right. It won't be long before you start talking."

He bent at the waist and reached to the floor to his left. His fingers came into contact with a coil of weighty chain. It was always there, a comforting friend. He lifted it then wrapped one end around his hand. Once he had a firm grip, he turned his hand into a fist and stepped towards the hanging men. His footsteps echoed, the chain clinked, and it seemed every muscle in their bodies tensed, right down to their toes.

"My name is Cricket. Pleased to make your acquaintance."

Briggs frowned.

"Oh, yes," Cricket said. "You may recall one of your colleagues at the graveyard telling you a little story. Mark, was it? The last time he saw me up close I had a red baseball cap on."

Realisation played out on Briggs' face.

"I asked him to dig and keep his mouth shut. He only obeyed one of my commands, hence this...situation. Unfortunate that he told you what had happened that night, but there you go. So many people tend to ignore me and have lived to regret it."

Briggs tugged at the chains. Useless to, really. He wasn't going anywhere.

"And you," Cricket addressed Oliver. "How do you feel about dying here?"

"Fuck you!" Oliver said, breaths snorting out of his nose.

Oh, a feisty fucker.

"What the hell do you want?" Oliver yelled, his voice going hoarse, the cords in his neck standing out.

"Don't, Oliver." Briggs looked sideways at him. "It isn't worth it."

"You're right." Cricket took another couple of steps forward and trailed the loose part of the chain through the fingers of his free hand. "It isn't. Fucking. Worth it. Because...in the end, I *always* get what I want."

"What *do* you want, eh?" Oliver asked. "Come on, ask us what we know. Ask us if we've shit ourselves ever since we were taken earlier. Ask us whether we want to live or die, even though you know you're going to kill us. Go on! *Ask us!*"

His last words came out on a scream, and it was clear he was running on adrenaline that would soon wear him out. Briggs, however, was playing it right, preserving his energy by remaining quiet and calm.

However they acted, they'd still get a whipping.

"I'll address the things you've said, because you've touched on everything I wanted to ask. Funny, that." Cricket smirked. "You know I dumped a body in the cemetery, and that's enough to get me put away if I ever land up in court. I'd say that yes, you've been shitting yourself. Your faces look gaunt. Fright tends to do that to a man."

86

He laughed, feeding the chain through his fingers again. "And I would say you want to live."

He flashed the chain out, the end catching Oliver's belly.

Oliver drew his knees up and screamed, the muscles in his arms bunching as though they'd burst through his skin. His eyes reduced to slits, and his mouth formed a skewed hole, his teeth bared and flashing in the light.

Cricket waited for him to lower his legs and shut up.

"That hurt, did it?" he asked casually.

"You fucking *bastard!*" Briggs shouted, his face a contortion of red anger. "What the fuck has he ever done to you to deserve *that?*"

"What has he ever"—Cricket flicked the chain at Briggs' thighs—"done?"

His body reacted the same way as Oliver's, except he didn't utter any sound but a strangled groan.

Ah, someone who'd rather suffer in near silence than let me know he's hurting.

"You gave me a sleepless night, that's what you've *done,*" Cricket said. "I don't like that. A good night's rest is the order of my fucking day, you wanker." He flicked the chain at Briggs—again, again, again—hitting him on the shins of his drawn-up legs. He wanted to break the little shit, get him screaming, begging for him to stop.

Briggs clenched his fists around the chains holding him in place and gritted his teeth, sweat breaking out on his forehead and dribbling down his temples. "Arsehole. You're a fucking *arsehole!*"

He opened his eyes, and they bulged, the veins in his neck standing out beneath the skin. He lowered his legs, wincing, probably bracing himself for another flick to his thighs.

Oliver looked on, momentarily stunned.

Cricket roared and lunged forward, lashing at them with the chain, striking harder. Tears streamed down their faces, and sobs tore from their throats, but they held firm. They fucking held firm.

"You bastards," Cricket raged, slashing until his shoulder ached.

Spent and out of breath, he stepped backwards, dropping the chain to its usual place on the floor. He panted. Blood dripped down their skin from the open welts he'd given them.

What the hell was he going to do with them?

Turning his back, he flicked off the light then climbed the stairs in the darkness, taking a moment at the top to hike in a deep breath and calm himself. Never had he encountered something like that with such a fierce beating. People just didn't remain *strong* like they had— not even the most hardened criminals.

He opened the door. Stepped into the corridor, intent on leaving them hanging there all night. Locked them in. He strode down the hallway, unlocked the farthest door, then entered the kitchen, which was now filled with his employees enjoying a Chinese takeaway. Some sat at the breakfast bar and others leant against the centre island.

The stink of the food churned his stomach.

"Everything all right, boss?" Denzell asked from the corner by the sink unit, a slight frown creasing his brow.

"Yeah." Cricket avoided looking at his men and made for the other doorway to the foyer. "It will be once I've had a proper night's sleep. At last. Leave our new guests exactly where they are. I'll deal with them in the morning."

"Right, boss," Denzell said. "Oh, and... Your promise... Can I go out tonight now?"

It took a moment for Cricket to understand what Denzell meant. Then he remembered he'd offered him a reward if he came back tonight, if he didn't run. "Oh, yes. Back by at least three a.m., though. You've earned your night on the town, but tomorrow night's a big one—don't forget that."

"Cheers."

Cricket stopped at the door and stared at his men. Denzell looked up from the plate he held, noodles on a fork poised midair, and raised his eyebrows in question.

"On second thought, take the cellar two down from the chains when you get back from wherever it is you're going tonight," Cricket said.

Without waiting to see any surprise on Denzell's face, Cricket swivelled and veered left into the living room. He went straight to the globe-topped drink's cabinet to pour a large measure of brandy.

"Stephen," he said quietly. "I need Stephen. But first I need to nip out. I want fresh air and some time to my fucking self."

CHAPTER ELEVEN

Stephen's nerves stretched taut, and his fear had escalated to him being beyond scared. All day he'd been thinking of how he could escape, what he could do to get word to the police—or anyone at all. He'd come up with a solution. What he was about to do could end his life if he got found out. There weren't enough words to describe the apprehension inside him. It eased somewhat as he sat on the window seat in his room, staring at the chest of drawers beside his bed.

Yeah, Cricket would kill him if he knew.

But Cricket and his men seemed to have gone out again. To the pub after a long day? There had been the distinct waft of Chinese takeaway at one point, and the sounds of men talking and laughing. Stephen hadn't bothered going down to join them. He wasn't hungry.

Although reticent to leave his sanctuary, he inched out of it anyway, wanting to do something to keep his mind occupied. He'd been thinking too much about his mum, his brother, and depression was creeping into the edges of his mind. His body seemed heavy, too, as though the burden of his situation was a weighty thing that stood on his shoulders.

On the landing, he crept to the top of the wide staircase, stopping short upon hearing voices. Lowering to his haunches, he sidled backwards a bit and hoped the shadows kept him hidden.

Two men stood leaning against the waist-high oak sideboard on the wall opposite the stairs in the foyer, which, Stephen guessed, was used only to show off the expensive crystal ornaments on top. A swan. A bowl containing potpourri. An empty vase.

"I don't envy Jonathan and Kevin tonight," one of the men said, his brown hair greying at the temples. He was stocky, clean-shaven, and looked like anyone's kindly dad. Not menacing at all.

"Me neither, but I'm glad it isn't us. Fucking nippy out there." The second man, red hair shaved to a couple of millimetres, rubbed the large bald spot on his crown.

"Reckon they'll get another one in time?" Stocky picked at a hangnail.

"Dunno, but they'd better."

"Pain up the arse that one of them hanged himself." Emotions streaked across Stocky's face. Sorrow?

"Yeah, puts a bit of pressure on to make sure there are ten of them by tomorrow night."

Oddly, they both chuckled, despite the vile conversation. Stephen detected a bit of fear there. Redhead paced, his thick-soled boots squeaking on the polished tile. Stocky pushed off the sideboard. The crystal ornaments wobbled. He moved to the front door, peering through the peephole.

"I'm bored shitless," Redhead said. "Reckon that Stephen bloke is asleep?"

"I would be if Cricket kept me up all night like he does with his favourites." Stocky laughed.

"I'll go and check. If he is, we can knob off into the living room. Play cards."

Redhead walked towards the stairs, and Stephen got up as quietly as he could. His heart pounded violently. He scurried into his room, leaving the door ajar. Scrabbling onto the bed, he lay in the foetal position, closed his eyes, and concentrated on making his breaths heavy, as though he was, indeed, asleep.

Redhead's boots clonked up the stairs. Stephen's heartbeat went haywire, and he willed himself to calm down.

Breathe slowly. Just...breathe.

His door creaked, and it took everything in him to stop his eyelids flickering. His pulse thundered in his ears, and a ripple of shudders went up his spine. It seemed a long time passed with him shitting bricks and wishing the man would go away, then Redhead stomped off.

Stephen waited a while longer then opened his eyes and looked at the doorway. For all he knew, Redhead still stood behind that door, tricking him into thinking he'd gone. Although scared, Stephen got off the bed. He tiptoed to the door. If Redhead *was* on the other side, Stephen would just say he was going to the bathroom.

Redhead wasn't there.

On the landing, Stephen stopped to listen for a moment then moved forward to the newel post. Opposite was another landing. Matching doors stood closed. What was behind them? He opened the first four doors, finding more bedrooms. At the fifth, he paused. Redhead's and Stocky's voices filtered up to him, raucous and coarse, the men ribbing one another in the living room.

Stephen turned the handle. He stared down a long corridor and walked the length until he reached the door at the end.

What if it's locked?

It wasn't. Another corridor running across like a T-junction was on the other side. A second set of ten doors. He checked the rooms—all full of beds except one, which was a long and thin office that stretched so far back he couldn't make out what the pictures were on the walls down there. He glanced about. Several desks with computers, printers, and scanners. It seemed like a control room of some sort, a place he really shouldn't be, but the sixth sense which had urged him to come here prodded him again.

Computers. Information. Knowledge. Power.

He strode to the computer nearest to him and booted it up. Thanked his lucky stars he knew his way around a PC—in more ways than one. Putting Redhead and Stocky out of his mind and praying luck was on his side, he breezed past the password obstacle and accessed the desktop. There were no file icons, just ones for Chrome, Adobe Reader, and some firewall application.

Stephen laughed quietly at the latter. He'd have thought Cricket would have chosen a better firewall, what with the important information these computers must hold. Tapping the keys and working the mouse, he found what he sought. A file consisting of names and addresses, payment details, everything the police would need to track down each person who had ever bought a homeless man from Cricket.

He tried Chrome. A message came up saying the computer wasn't connected to the Internet.

He had no way of getting the damning information to anyone. He searched for a memory stick.

Nothing.

Shit.

What else was there but for him to return to his bed?

Once he was back at the landing outside his room, Redhead's and Stocky's loud laughter snaked up the stairs. Stephen opened the door.

The hinges shrieked.

The men's laughter stopped.

"What was that?" Stocky.

"Fuck knows. Reckon Stephen's awake?" Redhead.

"Go and check."

Fuck!

Panicked beyond measure, Stephen had no choice but to lunge inside his room.

Footsteps smacked on the foyer floor. Donked on the stairs.

Stephen had enough time to leave the door ajar then clamber onto his bed. He *didn't* have time to steady his breathing—the footsteps were on the landing.

Holding air in his lungs, eyes closed, he waited for one of the men to burst in. The door creaked a little—he guessed it had been opened a bit.

Oh God. I'm caught. I'm—

The footsteps set up again, changing beat—the man going downstairs. Stephen released the air through pursed lips, tears stinging, and quietly got off the bed. At his door, he strained to hear any conversation from Redhead and Stocky. Soft murmurs reached him, then a burst of laughter.

Relief spread through him. His limbs shook, and his pulse banged in his throat.

Once the adrenaline rush had dispersed and he felt reasonably normal, he went downstairs. At the living room doorway, he nodded to Stocky and Redhead, who sat on a sofa, cards spread out on a coffee table before them.

"Just getting something to eat. Do you want anything?" he asked.

The men looked at one another.

"Yeah, why not," Stocky said. "A sandwich would be nice."

"Yeah, and a cuppa," Redhead added.

Stephen nodded again then made his way to the kitchen. He prepared what they'd asked for. His stomach growled, and he carried the men's food and drink into them on a tray. He set it on the coffee table beside the cards.

"Sounds like you need some food yourself. Your gut's got a lot to say for itself." Redhead reached for a ham salad sandwich. "Go on out there and eat. May as well take your fill while there's no other bugger around to beat you to it." He took a bite, stuffing the food to the side of his mouth, cheek bulging.

Stephen gave a tight smile. He returned to the kitchen. Devoured two sandwiches. Gulped down tea. It tasted like the cuppas his mum made, and he bit back a sob. Clamping his teeth on a knuckle, he paced in an attempt to give him something else to think about.

The door beside the breakfast bar snagged his attention, and he tried the handle again.

Locked.

Why did I think it would be otherwise?

The men yapped in the living room. Stephen quietly opened drawers. There had to be a landline phone here somewhere. *Had* to be. Or a spare mobile.

His search brought nothing but cutlery, serving spoons, and the usual kitchen paraphernalia.

Shit.

Mind working overtime, he tried to plan his best course of action while putting his plate and cup in the dishwasher.

No phones. No way of getting help unless one of them leaves a phone unguarded. I can't get out. I can't trust anyone here to take a message outside this house. I—

Dejected, he left the kitchen and passed the living room door.

Redhead called out, "Here, take these plates and cups out, will you?"

Stephen turned woodenly and gritted his teeth. He collected their things then went into the kitchen, trying not to ram the items in the dishwasher. Back in the foyer, he walked nonchalantly to the bottom of the stairs. He lifted his foot to take the first step—and the shower of gravel came, a vehicle parking outside the house.

No. Fuck, no. He can't be back yet. Please...

He faced the front door. It swung open to reveal Jonathan and Kevin, a black-haired, unconscious kid held between them.

"Here we go," Jonathan said. "Home sweet home."

"For a bit anyway." Kevin chuckled.

"What the fuck are you staring at?" Jonathan snapped, his gaze fixed on Stephen.

Gut rolling, Stephen climbed the stairs, the front door snicking shut, hating the sound of the men dragging the new arrival towards the kitchen. He remembered how that had felt when they'd done the same to him, how his heart had thundered and his eyes had itched with the fierce sting of tears. How he'd called for his mum and been laughed at.

'She isn't coming, twat.'

Back in his room, he slumped down on the window seat and remained there. Some of Cricket's men returned from wherever they'd been. He recalled earlier when one of them— Denzell, he thought—had arrived with two men who'd looked scared shitless when they'd got out from the back of the van.

He snapped out of his head at another set of headlights. So Cricket was back, too, hurtling up the drive in a red sports car.

A slice of moon hung, a broken shard of pearl in a sky of black satin. The house erupted with jovial chatter and the clinking of glasses.

The sound of Cricket's voice in the foyer churned Stephen's stomach.

The sight of that man, a few moments later, standing in his bedroom doorway, almost had him being sick.

CHAPTER TWELVE

Denzell was a wily bastard as a kid and a wily bastard now.

He couldn't wait to get the fuck out of this shit.

When Cricket's men had had picked him up that night six months ago, he'd been the first to admit he'd messed up. His decision to leave home at fifteen had been an easy one. No kid liked living in a house where abuse was the norm and you didn't bat an eyelid at going hungry. Four months after his fifteenth birthday, his father had beaten him one time too many, and Denzell had stuffed a blanket and a change of clothes into a rucksack, raided his mum's drug money tin, and fucked off.

A sad aspect had been leaving his grandad behind—the man who'd tried to stop the beatings and bad treatment for as far back as Denzell could remember.

He did wonder, though, why Grandad hadn't informed the police about his grandsons who'd endured more neglect than any kids had a right to put up with. But Grandad lived with them, cruelty dished out to him, too, and Denzell supposed the old fella's self-esteem had been stripped away along with his dignity and sense of what was right.

Life was a bitch and then some.

Leaving his little brother, Isaac, had been tough, too, but Denzell had made an anonymous phone call to the police about his mum and dad and hoped the coppers had acted on it. He hadn't given his name, had just said there was a teenage boy living in Montgomery Lane who needed rescuing from his parents.

It was the best he could do.

Denzell's life had formed a pattern after a few weeks of trial and error living rough. He'd spent his days asleep in hidden alleyways, beneath bypasses, and his nights awake roaming Central London. It was safer that way. Forced to share his arse with whoever paid for it just so he could eat, he'd learned to judge who posed a threat and who didn't. The hours of walking the night-time streets had seen him grow into a burly sod over the years, and despite wanting a better life, with a wife, two kids, and, let's go for it, a bloody dog, he'd remained homeless.

It was a bit of a bugger to get out of.

He reflected that his judgment hadn't been sound after all—or as sound as he'd thought it was anyway. Jonathan and Kevin had approached him on a night where the rain had lashed down and the wind had blown more than the cobwebs away. When he thought about it now, he wondered why they'd chosen him, as big as he was, when the men who were usually brought back were slender, waif-like. Maybe they'd needed him to make up the numbers.

Denzell was cold, depressed, and possibly at his most vulnerable. Jonathan and Kevin seemed friendly enough, asking if he was for rent, that they'd pay triple if he engaged in a threesome. That meant enough money to spend the night in a cheap hotel or B&B. Have a bath or shower. Get a comfortable bed with dry sheets and a quilt.

Denzell agreed and followed them down the street, bunching his hands at his sides in case he needed to defend himself. He should listen to his instincts, that tiny worm of unease that flourished in his gut the minute they led him down an alley filled with rubbish and a rat the size of a Jack Russell.

But the money and the thought of that hotel erased the doubt.

At the end of the alley, a black van idled, grey exhaust fumes billowing into the air, same as the rapid breaths from Denzell's mouth. He glanced back, judging how quickly he could run before the men ahead caught him legging it.

A proper bed. A bath...

Denzell continued to follow.

Once at the van, Jonathan opened a back door then held his hand up in a gesture for Denzell to climb inside. Again, the worm of unease wiggled, and again Denzell ignored it.

He entered the van.

They travelled out of inner London. The dense bright lights tapered off, the spread-out twinkles of the outlying homes taking their place, and that worm turned into a fuck-off anaconda.

"Hey!" Denzell said from his seat on the bench, staring at Jonathan and Kevin through the metal grate. "Where are we going?"

"Home, mate." Kevin chuckled.

"What, to your place?" Denzell bit his bottom lip.

"No, it doesn't belong to us," Jonathan said, "but it'll be home to you for the next six months. Now shut the fuck up."

Jonathan drove faster.

Denzell remained silent, not through fear but to gather his wits. He had no fucking clue why he had to stay wherever for the next six months—why six months was even the stated number—but he had a good idea of the duties he'd have to perform.

After travelling for a while, Denzell sifting through his options along the way, the van arrived at a mansion in the countryside. They escorted him inside, gave him 'the cellar treatment', and at the point where Cricket usually tested the 'cargo', Denzell got a break.

"He's too big," Cricket said. "What the fuck were you playing at picking someone like him?"

Cricket then offered Denzell a job.

Of course, he took it. He'd have to pretend to enjoy what they asked him to do. Feeding the abducted men, making sure none of them did themselves any harm. Their skin had to remain unblemished—no bruises, no cold sores, nothing. At first the rooms were empty, and Denzell had been informed he was the first pick-up since the last batch had been auctioned off. He had a few seconds to wonder what that meant, then Cricket informed him that over a period of time they collected ten lads and brought them here.

Over the next six months, they were primed for sale, incarcerated in those rooms, no contact with anyone except when Denzell fed them, made sure they were clean, gave them fresh sheets, dropped off their clean washing.

He talked to the young men. Eased their fears without telling them what life held in store. Denzell couldn't risk any one of those lads blabbing. It was hard not to become attached. Some were so fucking distraught to begin with that he had a difficult time not revealing his plans.

He couldn't risk it. To get them to safety meant playing Cricket's game, following the rules.

Cricket had a smooth operation going on. Maybe some of those lads would get a better life if they were purchased—those who'd led a life like Denzell had prior to coming here—but surely being out on the street was a safer bet. Then again, through the friends Denzell had made while living in the gutters, he'd heard tales that even good foster parents and care homes were rare.

What the fuck is the world coming to?

Sickened, he vowed to work his arse off for Cricket, gain his trust quickly—in time to release the ten lads currently in residence.

Tomorrow night they'd be auctioned if his plan went wrong.

Two months into his new job, he'd contemplated fucking off, driving up country to Scotland, starting again there. But the thought of abandoning all those captured men...

He couldn't do it.

Before he'd picked up the old man this morning, that editor, he'd telephoned the police and asked to speak to a detective he knew from the times he'd been nicked for 'soliciting', a policeman who concerned himself with Denzell's welfare for no reason Denzell could fathom. Maybe the bloke was just a good man. Maybe he saw something in Denzell's eyes—an abused kid living the best way he knew how, still abused as an adult but on his own terms. Detective Fairbrother had made it his business to appear on Denzell's turf a couple of nights a week, asking if he'd eaten, whether he'd made enough money to survive another day.

Fairbrother had come on the phone line, his tone jovial but with a tinge of unease. Denzell didn't want to fully believe this fella really *did* give a shit, but the concern in the policeman's voice had warmed him, gave him hope that what he was about to do would change more than the ten innocent lives in those rooms.

Quickly explaining his plans, Denzell had secured Fairbrother's attention and support and also his mobile number. Scribbling the digits on a pad, Denzell had explained why the police couldn't storm the mansion now—he wanted the purchasers caught, too.

He'd agreed to phone Fairbrother when he had further news or needed a little help along the way. When he'd had a spare second with no one around, he'd sent another text to the copper, asking him to meet him tonight.

You're nearly there. All this will have been worth it.

Now, with a belly full of Chinese noodles churning in his stomach, he drove one of the many black vans Cricket owned. He released a heavy breath, his heart ticking fast and his hands shaky. What he was about to do would either sign his death warrant or get him arrested. He just had to pray Fairbrother stuck to his promise of only moving in on Denzell's command.

On this trip to a village a few miles away, he thought about his day. It'd been a long one, and he was tired, but after tomorrow night he hoped he could sleep the sleep of the dead—though not literally. He was so tense his neck muscles ached like a bastard, and his head was foggy. Still, he'd sworn he'd see this through to its conclusion and he wasn't about to back out now.

He'd hated punching that editor. It had been akin to hitting Grandad, but a necessary evil, a means to an end. Fairbrother had promised his colleague would drive to the other end of Fountain Street and wait for the old man once he'd been released, putting the poor sod's mind at rest that he wouldn't have to live in fear for the rest of his life, that the police were aware of what had happened.

With the editor gone and the journey around London to pass the time well underway, Denzell had heard every word between Briggs and Oliver. Several times he'd had to bite his tongue to hold back from telling them that everything would be all right, that they didn't have to worry. But for all he knew, the van was bugged. Also, 'the cellar treatment' was coming their way, and most men gave up information once the chain struck their flesh.

Denzell hadn't been able to risk it.

Shaking his head, clearing it of the past and focusing on what he had to do now, he turned into a countryside pub car park, The Red Lion, and left the van in plain sight. He could have been followed by a couple of Cricket's men. He knew the deviousness of the bloke, maybe hadn't quite earned the sadistic wanker's trust, and meeting with Fairbrother in such a public place wasn't an option.

Which was why he wasn't meeting him here.

Denzell entered the pub and sat by a window facing the car park, non-alcoholic pint in one hand, the other resting along the sill. He had a good view of outside and spotted one of Cricket's cars straight away—a green Fiat Punto, two shadowed figures inside.

They can sit there as long as they fucking like.

They remained in there for two hours then slowly peeled away, the Fiat's taillights fading into the darkness of the road leading back to Cricket's place. Denzell sat for another hour, casually glancing through the window every so often and scoping out the cars.

They were all empty.

His instinct telling him it was safe to move, he dialled Fairbrother's number and waited for him to answer. The detective picked up on the second ring and agreed to meet at The Spotted Duck in the village of Framcott. On the way there, Denzell kept glancing in the rearview mirror to check for any tails and went through everything he needed to tell the copper.

Framcott's sign glowed from his headlights all too soon, and his gut clenched. Blowing out through tight lips to steady his pattering heart and rapid pulse, he drove into the pub's car park, found a spot to leave the van, and cut the engine. He sat for a moment, waiting for any traffic to drive past. It didn't. Telling himself he was doing the right thing, he exited and pushed the pub door wide, approaching the bar on legs that were a tad unsteady.

Again ordering a non-alcoholic beer, he finally chanced a look around the pub. Fairbrother sat in the far corner at a small round table beside a fireplace. The detective nodded a greeting, and, checking his surroundings again, Denzell walked over to take a seat.

"Fucking fair can of worms you've opened for me, Denzell." Fairbrother leant forward to rest his elbow on the table and cup his cheek in his hand.

Was that to shield his face from anyone who might be sitting outside?

Nice touch.

Fairbrother lowered his gaze to an A4 pad on the table. "I'll need the layout of the house. And the address."

Denzell took a sip of beer then placed the glass on a cardboard coaster. He took a pen from the inside pocket of his jacket and sketched the ground floor, paying specific attention to the door in the kitchen and the corridor beyond.

"This is where the lads are right now." He jabbed the nib on the pad. "But when you arrive— if everything goes all right—the lads will be in here." Denzell added more of the mansion's layout on the other side of the foyer, drawing the large dining room then The Viewing Room beside that. "A bloke called Jonathan usually mans the front door, and one called Kevin lords it over the back. In The Viewing Room, when you first go in, you'll see a row of chairs, the bidders sitting in them. Cricket will be there, too, plus some of his employees.

"On the opposite wall to the door, there's a massive two-way mirror. The lads will be taken in there one by one so the punters can see what's on offer." Denzell winced, adding more of the layout. "There's a door here, to the right of the mirror.

One of Cricket's men will be standing in front of it. Possibly armed. Behind that door is a corridor. First door on your left leads into the room behind the mirror. Second door on the left is the holding room where the lads are kept while they wait to be shown off."

Fairbrother sipped what looked like whiskey. He swallowed and grimaced. "And beyond that? Any rooms I should know about?"

"No, that's it." Denzell folded the page over. He got on with drawing the first floor. "Now, there's this kid called Stephen. He got picked up late—the other night—because one of the original ten managed to hang himself using his bedsheet." The memory of that man, nineteen years old and desperate, dangling from the ceiling light fitment, pierced Denzell's mind. The poor kid had partially ripped the sheet so he could tie it around, and he'd died before the fitment gave way. The fella had been found on the floor, chunks of ceiling plaster around him and dusting his hair.

Denzell blinked—damn tears—and cleared his throat. "But, um, Cricket kept Stephen for himself."

"So there are only nine kids going on show tomorrow night?"

"No. Jonathan and Kevin were meant to be picking another one up tonight. I'll meet him in the morning when I take in his breakfast, providing they find someone." Denzell's throat swelled with emotion. He took a swig of beer to ease the pain.

"Do you know any of these lads' names?" Fairbrother swirled the ice in his drink with his index finger. He seemed particularly interested in getting an answer.

"Yeah. Memorised them after I got to know them—but one won't tell me fuck all. You want the eight I know?"

"Please. Write them down. Their parents can be informed that we might have found their sons, depending whether they're the right men, if the parents even realise their sons are missing. Some don't file reports, you know."

Denzell nodded. "Yeah, I know. Like my situation."

Fairbrother shook his head. "It fucking amazes me how some parents don't give a shit." He stared through window, the side of his face still shielded.

"I'll just jot the names down then."

Fairbrother quickly returned his attention to the pad. It seemed as though he was holding his breath as Denzell wrote. When he'd written all he knew, Fairbrother slumped his shoulders and let out a shiver of air.

Denzell frowned. "Like I said, I don't know the name of the one who won't cough up info, or the new one yet. I can tell you his tomorrow at some point, *if* he tells me. I'll text you if I manage to find some time alone."

"All right." Fairbrother looked down at the pad as though wishing a name he'd clearly been hoping for would appear. "I can run these lads through the computer when I get back to the station. This is a hell of a thing you're doing here, Denzell. We've had our ears to the ground for a long time over Cricket, years, but we had no idea it was him

who was the brains behind this shit. We thought—
"

"He was into drugs? Yeah. He finds that funny." Denzell shook his head.

"So you brought two new men in today, you said in your text."

"Yeah. What about them?" Denzell asked.

"Older than the norm, aren't they?"

"How do you know?" Denzell wondered if Fairbrother had had him followed after all.

"I ran their names through the database when you told me who you'd collected. Why does Cricket want them?" Fairbrother smiled. "I mean, they can hardly be sold off as young men at their age."

"One of them, Briggs, worked at the cemetery and saw Cricket a couple of days ago. And the other, Oliver, well, he was picked up to be on the safe side. Briggs' best mate by all accounts. Cricket couldn't risk Briggs blabbing."

"I see. So has Cricket got plans for them?"

"They'll probably be killed once he gets information out of them. That's the way it usually goes."

"Fuck." Fairbrother smacked the side of his fist on the table.

What was going on? Was there more to this than he thought? Denzell didn't know, but it didn't matter anyway. So long as his plan went okay, he didn't much give a shit. "Listen, Cricket gave me the job of making sure an outside security team is in place tomorrow night. Think it's stupid myself, him not vetting who the security is, but then again, the less people who know what he's really up to, the better. I reckon that could be you and your lot, playing at being a security firm?"

Fairbrother nodded.

Denzell went on, "I'll open the gates for you because Cricket gave me that job for tomorrow night as well. If anything goes wrong, you'll have about an hour after the last bid before you need to really get a move on if you want to catch them. From listening to conversations over the past few months, I've gathered the bidders have a bit of a drink before they take their purchases home."

Fairbrother nodded again. "Celebrating. Fucking bastards."

"Oh, and Cricket usually leaves blokes strung up all night after 'the cellar treatment', but he wants me to take Briggs and Oliver down when I get back."

If I get back. If I haven't been watched.

"Is that significant, do you think?" Fairbrother asked.

"Could be. He gave me a job, didn't he? Maybe they'll get lucky and he'll offer them one."

"And that kid who hung himself?" Denzell shook his head. "What happened to him?"

"They buried him in the forest out the back. I'll show you when this is all over."

Denzell stood and, giving Fairbrother a nod, left the pub.

He hadn't asked what would happen to him when the police raided the mansion.

Going to prison for his part in Cricket's warped organisation was a million times better than the shit he'd been through in his life so far.

CHAPTER THIRTEEN

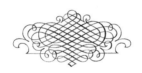

Langham's shoulders were burning. Even his armpits.

Everything fucking ached.

Hanging like this...he'd seen it in torture scenes on TV but had never quite got to grips with how much it hurt. Now, he knew *exactly* how much.

It was indescribable. Something he thought he wouldn't be able to tolerate.

Funny how the mind and body work so you can cope.

At first, the pain had been too much to handle. With every gripe, every spear of agony, he thought about how it felt and wallowed in it. But, as with a toothache, if he forgot about it, something else taking his attention, his mind not focusing on that Godawful throb, the pain went away.

He tried that again now, pushing his mind to another level, centring on images from the past or memories he cherished. Anything so he didn't feel.

It didn't work all the time.

Talking to Oliver wasn't an option either. Finding the words, or even the energy to speak them, brought on fresh bouts of anguish that ripped through him, jangling every nerve ending and magnifying the stress until he thought he'd pass out.

A mantra flowed through his head. *Think of something else, think of something else...*

As though the pain was a being that had the ability to hear, it raised its intensity a notch, forming itself into a monster that liked to torment and send a man insane. With each new level, he told himself he couldn't take any more. Not another second of this bastard shit. And every time he managed to tolerate it.

He'd heard somewhere that the human body and mind were able to transcend pain. He could only describe it as going into a trance, his soul rising from his body to hover above him, his shell left there, hanging. The part of him that processed pain, his *self*, was free of distress.

Or am I actually dead?

The second he'd thought that, his *self* zipped back into his body. The rush of discomfort stripped him of the ability to breathe, like someone was choking him.

He wanted to hear Oliver's voice, needed to in order to fully understand he wasn't alone. Oh, he knew Oliver was there all right, but in this darkness it was easy to forget. It stretched on for what seemed like miles yet closed in on him at the same time.

Langham inhaled a breath at last. "I'm..." His voice, just a whisper, broke through the seam of his dry lips. "I'm okay. I'm alive."

And he rose out of his body again, wondering if he'd passed out and this was what it felt like when you neared death. Did the *self* separate from the body, waiting in some kind of indeterminate state for the shell to give up? Did the *self* linger, just in case the body wanted it back?

He watched himself from a great height. His head bobbed, his chin dropping to his chest. There was no pain. Sleep, blessed sleep, had shooed it away for now.

He knew he dreamed, even though it seemed like he was awake inside a body and mind that had shut off for a while. He found himself at the graveside, staring down at a hole, Oliver underneath all that mud. He turned full circle to appraise his surroundings, uneasy that Cricket would return and catch him there.

He narrowed his eyes, seeking out any kind of movement in the foggy shadows of the place he'd worked undercover. Nothing appeared abnormal. Because he dreamed, he stood waiting for something weird to happen, for Oliver to burst out of the earth as a vampire or zombie, but the unnatural silence held everything suspended.

Abruptly, Oliver appeared beside him, unmarked and clean, and for a minute Langham tried to process how that had happened. He opened his mouth to tell him they were going to die, but Oliver became transparent, fading, blending with the mist. Quickly, Langham jumped into the open grave. He went down on his hands and knees, fingers claw-like, and dug at the earth.

He dug for a long time, deeper than the original grave. His fingers met with packed earth, nails getting broken, and he sat back, uncomprehending that Oliver wasn't there.

But he was here. I saw him. He stood beside me. What the hell does this mean? Is this how Oliver gets his information from spirit? Is this what the poor sod has to put up with when they contact him? Bullshit puzzles?

How Langham got out of the grave he didn't know. One minute he was in it, the next he stood beside it again, his hands clean, standing out bright white by the light of the moon.

I'm dreaming. Must remember I'm dreaming.

Confused, he wandered towards the old shed used to store tools and make tea on their breaks.

Inside didn't look the same. The chair had gone, replaced with a stone coffin, the lid askew. A blackboard on an easel stood in place of the fridge, and behind it was a small window. Spiders had made themselves at home in layers of dust, their webs thick, swathes of candyfloss.

A shuffle sounded beside him, and he automatically glanced at the open door. The mist had thickened, forming an opaque wall that prevented him from seeing into the graveyard. He slammed the door on it, the mist's sudden density spooking him, as though it held some meaning he had yet to grasp. He locked the door, moved towards the blackboard. A spider scuttled down his arm, and he jumped back, flicking his wrist to get the critter to fall off. It gripped with long legs, refusing to budge, and as he stared at it, the creature grew. He brushed it off, stamping on the bastard once it hit the floor.

It might have been an omen for him not to look at the blackboard.

Swallowing, he moved forward again, omen or not.

It had writing on it: OLIVER'S GONE.

Langham struggled to wake up, frantic that Oliver had died hanging beside him, while he'd been dreaming, dicking about with spiders and blackboards.

The full veil of sleep lifted, transporting him back to reality. He jerked, the manacles ripping into his flesh, but it didn't matter. Even the dribble of hot blood flowing down his arms failed to make any significant impact.

Then oblivion gripped him again, dragging him down into a dark pit.

CHAPTER FOURTEEN

*O*liver drifted somewhere he didn't recognise. *This field, full of buttercups, the grass clipped short, reminiscent of a football pitch, was an alien place. It stretched for miles, surrounded by white clouds that stopped abruptly at the horizon, no blue sky in sight. But it was daytime, he got the sense of*

that, the light too natural to be any form of man-made illumination.

He turned in a circle. Which direction to take? It didn't much matter *which way he went—it all looked the same—so he limped forward, the flowers brushing the tops of his bare feet. He stared down at himself. The shock of welts and bruises over his naked body brought with it a prodding memory that somewhere else, all was not well with him. He stood still, head cocked, waiting for images to form in his mind, ones he could latch on to and reel in until they formed a bigger picture.*

Naked. Welts. Bruises. Where did he get them from?

He lifted his arms in front of him, studying the circles of sore skin around his wrists.

"Please, spirit, tell me why I'm like this. Why I'm here. If you've got something to tell me, just get on with it. None of this weird visual shit."

No response.

He hobbled on, his destination pulling him one way, his mind the other. He sensed a large chunk of information was missing, information he needed to know.

He stopped again at a rippling tinkle.

What the fuck was that?

Spinning in a circle—shit, his ankle hurt—he hoped to see something other than the field and clouds, some chink in the green, yellow, and white expanse that could tell him where that tinkle had come from.

Nothing greeted him but the same view.

"This way, Oliver..."

The male voice held familiarity, as though he should recognise who'd spoken. But it hadn't quite sounded like he'd thought it should. Reedy. Indistinct. He turned again, his eyes hurting from the brightness of the clouds, which glowed, as if a great lamp had been switched on behind them. He squinted to protect his eyes from the glare.

"Come on. This way."

The voice had come from behind him, and he whirled quickly, coming face to face with Langham, who smiled, head tilted, eyes twinkling from the light.

"I'm dreaming," Langham said. "I know I am, and shit, it's good to see you, man. I followed you here."

"Where are we?" Oliver asked.

"I wasn't sure at first. But I think we're dying. Shit, we're dying." Langham stilled, as though a third party had spoken. "This way." He guided Oliver forward.

Oliver dug his heels into the grass. "No. I don't want to die. Not yet. We have to save those lads, and then there are other cases in the future. There's too much we need to do."

The tinkle floated again, louder this time, as though a chain was being jerked frantically.

The grass rustled.

"We can't stay here." Oliver ran the other way, instinct telling him where to go. "Come on. Hurry up!"

The clouds darkened on the horizon, grey rising at first, then black forming underneath, thick, angry stripes. Oliver sped on—the blackness was where they needed to be. A fierce wind blew from out of nowhere, jostling him as if it wanted to start a fight. He shoved against it, hair pushing back from his face, the skin on his cheeks rippling with the force. Hail pelted down, great slanting rods of it, obscuring his vision. Each rod was pointy-tipped, scratching at his cheeks with unseen fingernails.

The hail continued to smack him, a chastisement he didn't deserve. He glanced back at the white clouds and Langham still standing, his arm outstretched. The scenery there was untouched by the storm, the light still bright, Langham unaffected by the spiteful wind. A momentary feeling of goodness slipped through Oliver. But it wasn't strong enough for him to return to Langham. The darkness called louder, his whole being taut and buzzing with the knowledge that if he just reached that pitch horizon, then everything would be okay.

He turned away from Langham, facing the storm once more.

"Come back, Oliver," Langham called.

Oliver imagined him smiling, beckoning with his hand.

That hand...did it have the ability to rein him in? The wind tried to push him backwards, an accomplice to the hand he was sure worked to tug him to the place where Langham stood.

Body-racking shards of agony speared Oliver's body, his ankle throbbing harder, his wrists feeling as though they were about to snap.

"Wait!" Langham shouted.

A whooshing sensation shunted Oliver forward, but he managed to turn and hold out a hand.

Langham grabbed it, and they fell into nothing, hanging midair, suspended in pain and confusion.

Oliver's heart rate soared, and he battled to breathe through the panic.

Jolting to a stop, though still suspended, he fought to take in air.

Langham stared at him. "Talk to me, Oliver. For fuck's sake, answer me!"

Oliver finally sucked in a huge breath, his throat dry, his head pounding. "Langham?"

"Oh, thank *fuck* for that. I had a dream," Langham said, "that we were dying. I was happy to go, but you wanted to come back and—"

"You followed me."

"How do you know that?" Langham asked. "Oh Jesus. Did you get told by spirit?"

"No," Oliver said, understanding flooding him. "We had the same dream. Do you realise what that means?"

Langham's mouth dropped open.

"We connected," Oliver said. "We connected via our minds."

CHAPTER FIFTEEN

Cricket lay in bed, flat on his back and staring at the ceiling. Tonight should have been the night he got the first good sleep in a long time, but still a decent rest evaded him. He should have just had those men hanging in the cellar offed, got Jonathan or Kevin to kill the motherfuckers and been done with it. The vicious whipping with the chain had just been something to assuage Cricket's anger.

He'd built his life up, having been a street kid himself for a while in his mid-teens. He wanted to prove that people from a broken home *could* get somewhere if they put their minds to it. Helping those lads downstairs have better lives than they'd had previously pleased him no end, even though he made out he didn't give a fuck about them.

He did a good thing.

Cricket thought back to his childhood, one where his mother hadn't cared about him much. He hated her yet loved her just the same. He sighed and blinked hard.

His eyes itched.

He'd grown older and asked himself how he could love and hate someone in equal measure. By his early teens, he'd acted out at school, fucked about on the streets causing trouble, got in with a bad crowd. But that bad crowd had shown him how to become a runner, and he'd peddled drugs at night. This new way of life had given him a thirst for better things, showed him he could make it on his own without his mother. And he had once Parker picked him up off the street and took him to his home. To the home Cricket now owned.

He'd become Parker's pet, trusted with the ins and outs of the trafficking business as Cricket had grown from boy to man. And despite Parker preferring younger men, once Cricket had arrived on the scene, Parker hadn't taken another lover.

Cricket had loved him to some degree, but not enough to stop him from killing the old fucker to take over his patch once he'd written his will in Cricket's favour.

Ah, I've been a bastard in my time.

He wasn't getting any younger. He needed the kind of love he'd given Parker. Companionship.

Was Stephen his salvation or just another notch in his bedpost?

Cricket moved to get out of bed and reach for his mobile, but he couldn't bring himself to give the order to kill the hanging men. He flopped back onto the pillow, a huff of air shunting out of him. Maybe he ought to get Stephen in here. Cricket could tell him a story until Stephen fell asleep. Or explain what he needed from him. Hate and love, love and hate. Perhaps the lad would get it then, realise he had everything at his disposal if he'd only just love Cricket for being Cricket. Hate him for being him.

They were simple, his needs. He was a fuck-up, really, no doubt about that, but—

"Sod it. What am I going to do about those two down there?"

His voice, a whisper, sounded so amplified in the quiet. Most of the household had retired—he'd counted their footsteps as they'd gone to their rooms one by one—and he had no reason now *not* to fall into a sound sleep, except for his roiling emotions. Denzell had returned from his spell at the pub, like Cricket knew he would, his rumbling voice announcing to Jonathan in the foyer that he needed to cut the cellar men loose before he went to bed. He had yet to come up the stairs and go to his room, but it wouldn't be long.

Earlier, Cricket had instructed two underlings to follow Denzell to whatever pub he went to, though he hadn't expected Denzell to betray him, not really. Still, it didn't do to become lax with his staff. A first outing after being kept under strict supervision for six months sent some men off their rocker, and even today collecting Briggs and Oliver had been a big test. But the van had been tracked every step of the way, so if Denzell *had* taken it into his head to do a runner, he'd have been rounded up pretty sharpish.

Denzell knew his place, was grateful for what Cricket did for him, and he stood to become Cricket's right-hand man if he played his cards right. Another six months would see just that happening if Denzell continued in the vein he had. Cricket had a few more tests to put him through first, but the young bloke would pass them.

A good man, Denzell.

Cricket closed his eyes, thinking about tomorrow night. Security would be stepped up. He had outside contractors coming in to guard the immediate grounds—he must confirm with Denzell whether he'd done as he was told on that. Cricket couldn't believe he'd forgotten to check. He trusted Denzell enough to choose the right team.

Irked with himself, he threw the quilt back. Padded towards the door. Grabbed his dressing gown to cover his nakedness. He made his way in the dark downstairs, squinting in the light spilling into the foyer from the kitchen.

Denzell sat at the breakfast bar, a glass of orange juice before him and a newspaper spread out on the marble surface.

"Still up, Denzell?" Cricket approached him.

Denzell turned and smiled. "Yeah. All right, boss?"

"Enjoy your evening?" Cricket placed one hand on the breakfast bar, the other on Denzell's shoulder.

"Yeah. Was good to get out. Thanks."

Studying the man's face for signs of deception, Cricket found none and nodded. "Where did you go?"

"That pub up the road a bit. The Red Lion."

"Nice and quiet, was it?" Cricket squeezed Denzell's shoulder.

"Yeah. Enjoyed a couple of drinks. Bit of time to myself." Denzell nodded. "Yeah, it was fucking all right, actually."

Cricket patted his back. Hard. Just to let him know he was still being watched. "Fucking brilliant. Did you let them two ponces downstairs off the hook?"

Denzell laughed, gesturing to the newspaper. "Yeah. Was just having a gander at what's been going on in the world before I head up to bed."

"Right. I meant to ask, did you sort the security out for tomorrow night like I asked?" Cricket didn't doubt the man for a minute, but he needed to hear it just the same.

"Yep. Twenty of them." Denzell took a sip of his orange juice.

"Brilliant bloke, you are. Right, I'm off to bed. Need my sleep before I deal with those two tomorrow." Cricket jerked his head in the direction of the white corridor. "Know what I mean?" He sighed dramatically and left Denzell to his reading.

CHAPTER SIXTEEN

Denzell waited until he imagined Cricket's bedroom door had closed then released the breath he'd held. What had he been questioning him for?

Did I fuck up somewhere? Did someone see me with Fairbrother?

Another thought struck him—an unpleasant one.

Is Fairbrother in Cricket's pocket?

"Shit," he whispered, his whole body going cold.

He consoled himself with the fact he'd known Fairbrother well before he'd known Cricket. And Fairbrother appeared a good sort.

Yet Denzell remained uneasy. He wouldn't put it past Cricket to keep him under the false illusion that everything was hunky fucking dory when it bloody well wasn't. He'd have to watch himself now, watch Cricket and his men more carefully for any signs they suspected him of double-crossing them.

Fuck. That's all I need at the moment. I'm so close to getting these lads back home.

The thought of them had him contemplating going to see the latest one. It would be easier to find out his name now, while the house was quiet and no one was around to know he'd spent longer in his room than the others in the morning.

Reckon he needs to see a friendly face.

Denzell took out a plastic cup they used specifically for the lads and filled it with orange juice from the fridge. In a burst of daring, he prepared a sandwich—cheese and ham on brown bread with a little salad on the side—then used his keys to open the door beside the breakfast bar. He went into the corridor and lowered the tray to the floor. Back at the door to the kitchen, he locked it—Cricket would go ballistic if he left it open and the kid managed to get past him and into the house—then lifted the tray again. The lad would

134

be in room five, which had stood empty since…yeah, since the other one had killed himself.

He knocked softly. No response. He held the tray in one hand and unlocked the door with the other. Going inside, he took in the sight of a naked, black-haired young man bathed in the shaft of light streaking in from the corridor. He was curled up on the bed, above the quilt, his back to the door.

Denzell put the tray on a chest of drawers beside the door. Locked up. Pocketing the keys, he walked over to the bed. "Hey. You all right?"

Fucking stupid question. Of course he's not all right. Look at him shaking. He's shitting himself.

Not for the first time since he'd arrived here, anger sped through him until he thought he'd shout out his frustration at having to wait until tomorrow night to save these men. But at least it was tomorrow night. This one was lucky, only having to endure just over twenty-four hours in this place.

"I've brought you some food." Denzell sat on the edge of the bed.

The lad shook harder.

"Cheese and ham sandwich. Bit of salad. Some orange juice, too." He kept his voice calm. He'd be lucky to get this one's name out of him tonight. It usually took them a while to trust him, to realise he wasn't going to hurt them. "If you don't want to talk, that's all right. And if you want to eat facing the wall, that's all right, too."

The only response was a whimper.

Denzell rasped his palm over his beard. He'd be damn glad to shave it off once this nightmare was over. Growing it had been Cricket's idea. Apparently, Denzell looked more menacing with a face full of hair.

He tried again. "I can't leave the food here, mate. If you don't eat it, I'll have to take it away."

From where Denzell sat, it looked like the lad could do with a bite of grub. The ridge of his spine stood out, and his ribs reminded Denzell of a birdcage, pushing against the skin like that.

Fuck, this is awful. Years, bloody years this shit has been going on here.

The soles of the newbie's feet were rough, the heels bearing hard skin. This one hadn't been brought up pampered—or else he'd been on the streets a long time. If Denzell's plan didn't pan out, whoever bought this lad wouldn't be pleased about those feet.

"I was like you once," Denzell said gently. "Lying on one of these beds and wondering what was going to happen next. I'm the one who brings the food, changes the sheets, makes sure you're okay. Stuff like that."

No reaction except uneven breathing.

"Did the boss give you lemonade in the cellar?" Denzell winced at the thought of this kid being hurt in front of the other two men down there.

A barely imperceptible nod, but one was given all right.

"Did you tell him your name?"

Another nod.

"What's that then? I can't keep calling you 'mate', can I? Unless you want me to. And if that's

136

what you want, it's fine. I don't want you doing anything you don't want to."

Denzell didn't catch the answering whisper.

"What's that? You'll need to speak up a bit."

"Isaac," the boy said, his voice cracked. "I'm Isaac Croft."

Denzell's body seemed to hollow, like his bones had liquefied and everything inside him had disappeared. He instinctually reached out but remembered to hold back just before his fingers touched skin.

His brother's skin.

"Isaac?"

Turn around. Let me see your face. Show me you're not him, that this is something Cricket told you to say to me.

Fighting panic, anger, and burgeoning tears, Denzell took short little breaths to erase the many questions streaking through his mind. He needed a clear head. He needed to remain emotionless.

Fuck, it was hard to keep from crying, from grabbing that bony shoulder and forcing the lad to look at him, but he had to gain his trust. Couldn't let this fuck up months of hard work.

"I've got a brother called Isaac," Denzell said, keeping his tone light.

There was a released gasp.

Don't break down. Keep it together. "Haven't seen him in years. Don't reckon he'd even know me now. I miss him."

The newbie moved his head, just a tiny bit, to stare at Denzell with one eye over his shoulder. A dark-brown eye Denzell had seen fill with many a

137

tear after their mother had beaten the shit out of them. It *was* him.

Jesus fucking Christ.

Denzell leant over to see him better. "He looks a bit like you, actually. Funny, that, eh?" His heart thudded so hard he wondered if the lad could hear it. "I won't let anyone here hurt you, all right? Did the boss or his men...did they...do anything else to you in the cellar?"

Isaac eased around, embracing his shins, and settled on his other side so he faced the door. He nodded but looked as though he wasn't about to elaborate. Denzell drank in his features, and shit, it was like seeing himself at that age. His shins were covered in bruises, old and brown, some yellow-tinged.

From Mum's kicks? Dad's? Someone else's?

"My grandad's dead." Isaac stared at the door.

Aww, fuck. Fuck!

"I'm sorry to hear that, mate. Will your mum and dad be worried where you are?"

"Dunno. I left last year. When Grandad died." Isaac eyed the sandwich on the chest of drawers.

Why didn't I keep tabs on them? Why did I just leave and forget them all?

Denzell blinked hard.

Because you had to get yourself sorted, that's why. Come to terms with what happened to you.

"Do you want to eat?" Denzell asked.

He could take care of Isaac *now*, that's what mattered. Make up for what he hadn't done in the past.

Isaac nodded and sat up, groggy and not with it at all. He kept his knees pulled to his chest.

That fucking lemonade...

"Listen, mate. Isaac. Let me get you some clothes."

Denzell went to the drawers. He pulled out some jogging bottoms and a T-shirt. He held them out to Isaac, who reached up a thin arm, his wrist bones resembling two jutting marbles.

Denzell smiled. "I'll face the door so you can dress, yeah? Then you can eat."

He studied the wood grain of the door, eyes stinging. Should he try to hug his brother? Tell him what he had in mind?

Maybe this is a test from Cricket.

No, he'd remain on track, do everything as planned.

He took the tray. Handed it to Isaac. Stood by the door while the kid ate. Taking his phone from his pocket, he texted Fairbrother, his thumbs shaking as he pressed the buttons: *The new kid. He's my fucking brother.*

CHAPTER SEVENTEEN

Langham rested on a mattress in the darkness, Oliver beside him. Their left wrists were manacled, chains keeping them tethered to the wall of the alcove either side of them.

What was Oliver thinking? Why couldn't Langham find anything to say? Words failed him.

He kept going over what had happened in his mind and came up with a big ball of *what the fuck?*

He had no idea of the time. No idea how long they'd hung from the ceiling, how long they'd been on the mattress, or how long it would be before someone came back down to give them some more shit.

He reckoned they were in shock. Deep shock.

The sound of a door opening had Langham snapping his eyes open. Every muscle in his body screamed as the awareness of where he was smacked back into his mind. The mansion. A dank cellar, the smell of mould and damp permeating his nostrils.

While he dangled, he thought he was going crazy. That dream had been so weird, so real.

A faint shaft of light penetrated the darkness ahead, illuminating about three steps and a small square landing. The light faded to nothing, the blackness even more absolute than it'd been before. The door was relocked, the key scraping loud and ominous, and footsteps came towards them, strident and echoing.

Langham's heart thumped hard and fast, the fear inside him coming back right along with the pain of being stretched in a position no body had a right to be in. The skin at his wrists pinched from the manacles. Had the bones pierced through the skin? It felt like it. And if they had? Nothing he could do about it. He doubted either of them would be getting any medical attention.

He braced himself for that blinding light to come back on, for Cricket to be there behind the circle of brilliance, for the clink of the chain as he lifted it, ready to strike him and Oliver again. What the hell kind of person did that to another? Langham couldn't get over it. How had Cricket been getting away with this shit?

A softer light was switched on, in the right-hand corner, a low-watt bulb. The cone of peach-coloured light lit a circle on the rough cement floor, the darkness around it bleeding into the corona of shadows. Even that hurt his eyes, and it took a few seconds for his sight to become accustomed.

The person breathed loudly, sighed, as if they were tired or at a loss as to what to do. The breathing continued for a while. What was the person doing? Studying them? Building up a rage in order to whack them?

The not knowing was horrendous.

Langham no longer cared that he was naked, whether someone looked him up and down and found him wanting. And if whoever stood in front of them had a problem with the floor beneath Langham and Oliver being damp, then they could go and fuck themselves. They'd had to piss somewhere.

Langham opened his mouth to say something but wasn't sure what he should say. He suspected whatever he said would be ignored. Or he'd get punished for it.

"Please, will you just let Oliver go?" he whispered. "He won't say anything, and I'll stay here as insurance or whatever you want."

"You both have to stay," a man said.

143

Beardy. The big fucker walked towards them once he'd flicked another light on—one directly above—brighter than the one in the corner, sharp and intrusive on Langham's eyes. He shivered at the sight before him. Beardy appeared so sinister, the light only reaching the skin of his face. His beard melted into the darkness below, and it seemed as though only a forehead, eyes, and a nose hovered midair.

Langham expected Beardy to punch him in the face like he'd done to the editor, but the man just stood a couple of metres in front of them. His eyes held what looked like compassion, and it confused Langham. This bloke had been nothing but brusque with them when they'd been in his company, yet here he was, apparently sorry?

"I've been told to get you down," Beardy said. "I don't want any funny shit when I do either. It's better for you if you just let me lower you and attach you to another chain in the alcove back there." His face wavered. "Reckon anything's broken?"

Beardy sounded concerned. Did the man like his job or had he been forced to do it? That wouldn't surprise Langham in the slightest. Cricket was an arsehole.

"Broken?" Langham said. "Everything hurts. It tends to when you've been whipped with a fucking chain and left hanging for God knows how long, know what I mean?" He inwardly cursed himself for his outburst, but shit, he was going to die at some point anyway, so he might as well say what was on

144

his mind. "You'll soon see when you let us down, won't you? If we can walk, bonus, if we can't..."

"Right," Beardy said. "I'll let you down first." He stared at Langham.

"No. Let Oliver down. Please."

"Briggs," Oliver warned.

"Just let him get you down. I'll be all right for a while longer." As though his body wanted to prove him wrong, Langham's tendons and ligaments shrieked out their pain. He clenched his teeth and bunched his eyes closed.

"All right." Beardy reversed into the darkness. "I just need to use the mechanism back here, okay? Like I said, no shit when I let you down."

"I haven't got the strength for any," Oliver said.

Something clanked, and Oliver jolted. He cried out, neck tendons corded, and Langham contemplated swinging so he could stop his mate's body jerking from the chain going suddenly lax. Oliver slowly lowered to the floor. His body collapsed, the chains pooling, linked snakes. He rested on his side, arms still above his head, his back curved along the spotlight's circular edge.

"Oliver?" Langham said, the urgency in his voice putting a strain on his throat.

"I'm okay. Just need...a minute."

Beardy came back into view. "I'm going to take the manacles off. It's going to hurt, but I won't mean it to. And you'll need to lower your arms into their normal position really slowly, all right? When they've been up like that for so long... Just be glad you've been given some respite. People are normally left hanging overnight."

Langham couldn't imagine it.

Beardy hunkered down and unlocked the manacles at Oliver's wrists. Carefully, he opened the top halves—semi-circles of metal on oiled hinges. "Now, I'll leave you to take your wrists out. You know best when you're hurting, not me. You can rest when you need to. There's plenty of time."

Why was he being so nice? The calm before the storm?

Oliver's face scrunched up, and he lifted his hands from the restraints. Langham stared at the corner spotlight. A loud wail told him Oliver had lowered his arms, and he imagined the pain in the armpits.

"That's it, fella," Beardy said. "Reckon you can walk?"

"Yeah," Oliver answered.

Langham listened to the shuffles. A chain tinkled behind him, and he told himself to deal with the tenderness while he tried to swing around. He cried out, infinite darkness over his shoulder.

"Langham?" Oliver rasped. "What happened?"

"I'm fine. Just my wrists. You okay?"

"Yeah."

"He'll be grand," Beardy said. "Now, let me get you down, eh?"

Beardy's face appeared midair.

Langham stared down at him. "D'you like doing this kind of shit to people?"

Beardy blinked a couple of times and swallowed. "I'll just go back here and lower you."

He disappeared, the clank sounded, and Langham jerked the same way Oliver had. It took a lot to keep the building scream at bay. His feet met the concrete, and his legs gave way. He slumped, whacking his hip bone, his skin scuffing on the harsh concrete. Remembering what Beardy had instructed Oliver, Langham gritted his teeth. The manacles came loose, and it seemed to take an age for him to lift his wrists. And yeah, his armpits sang a strangled melody of warped and intense pain.

"Up you get," Beardy said. "There we go." He guided Langham into the darkness. "There's a mattress coming up ahead. I want you to sit on the end of it while I get the chain. I'm sorry I have to do that, you know, put a manacle back on but—"

Beardy had feelings?

"But what?" The mattress under Langham's arse was bliss.

"Nothing. Forget I said anything."

Although Langham wanted to press the man, his energy vanished. The manacle had gone around his wrist, giving a fresh burst of hurting, rubbing against the raw skin.

"Now, I've got to give you a drink." Beardy walked away, his back a momentary flash beneath the spotlight then disappearing into the darkness.

Beardy rustled and clonked about, and Langham caught a glimpse of him holding two glasses when he passed through the centre shaft of light.

"Here. Drink this."

Langham felt about in the air until his hand touched a glass. "What is it?"

"Lemonade," Beardy said. "Oliver, can you sit up without help?"

"Yeah."

More shuffles.

Langham sipped—blessed relief on his parched throat—the fluid oozing down into his stomach and pooling there.

"I need to get something," Beardy said, taking their glasses away.

He seemed to be gone a long time—time enough for Langham to get woozy, off on another planet. He tried to speak, ask Oliver whether he felt the same, but the words died on his tongue. As though listening through water, he made out the sound of Beardy coming back and a loud click. Something being opened? A flashlight came on, the beam pointing towards the contents of a briefcase. Langham couldn't see inside, the lid sticking up prevented it. Beardy, on his knees, fumbled around then gripped Langham's hand.

"I have to do this, understand? Doesn't mean I want to."

A sharp stab pricked Langham's arm, and he was vaguely aware of watching a needle float through the semi-darkness, back towards Beardy. Another one appeared in the man's hand, and he jabbed it in Oliver's arm.

Langham fell backwards, legs bent, feet on the concrete, his body too weighty to hold up. He closed his eyes, and the mattress undulated beneath him. He supposed Oliver had fallen back, too. Langham closed his eyes, the mattress jostling again. Stormy seas.

Then the questions came from Beardy, probing Langham's memory for answers. About seeing a man at the cemetery railings. Langham answered him without hesitation, his voice sluggish, drawn-

out, alien. Oliver's voice merged with his, and Beardy kept the enquiries coming. It wasn't long before Langham couldn't speak anymore, and he closed his eyes, not giving a shit where he was or what happened next.

Sometimes, you just had to give in and sleep.

CHAPTER EIGHTEEN

Cricket woke, the early morning light searing his retinas. He'd forgotten to close the damn curtains again last night. He'd left Stephen in his room, well-used and hating him a little more. No sign of love in the young man's eyes, but that was okay. It would come. Cricket had a feeling about it.

He had a lot to do today, preparing for the night ahead. Everyone knew the drill, had their specific tasks to perform, but he'd make sure his men were reminded all the same. It didn't do to solely rely on their loyalty and the memories of previous auction nights. One slip, and they'd all be fucked.

He padded to his en suite to switch the shower on. Instant heat billowed from the stall along with a cloud of grey steam. He got in. Thought about the coming sales. The punters expected him to be on the ball. If they thought he wasn't up to the job, they might not return to him time and again.

But they did, giving back the lads they'd previously bought for Cricket's men to dispose of. He didn't care that they were killed. Couldn't.

Once washed, he stepped out of the shower then dried off, the luxury of his expensive towel heaven on his skin.

Dressing and making sure his suit hung just so, he left his bedroom. He paused outside Stephen's door. Soft snores sounded, and he smiled that the young man had succumbed to sleep. Once they'd established a pattern and Stephen accepted his life was here, everything would slot into place. Cricket would get the sense of well-being he craved, and Stephen would be cherished like no other man alive.

He wanted to open the door, peek at the lad who stood to inherit his fortune. He curled his fingers around the handle. Turned it.

No, he couldn't allow for distractions. Not today. Tonight—once the auction had finished and the punters and boys were gone—was a different matter. The week off he allowed his men, the lull between the sale and the start of rounding up ten more boys, would be spent showing Stephen how wonderful life could be.

Cricket let the handle go and sniffed. Stephen's scent reached him. Then a click to his left got him curious. He walked along the landing. Jonathan came out of his room, suited and booted for the day ahead, and Cricket nodded, heading for the opposite landing.

In the corridor, he made his way to the office, ready to do his morning check. Did he detect Stephen's scent in here? Or was it because that beautiful aroma still lingered in his nostrils?

He cast his gaze around, making sure it was as he'd left it the previous morning. There had been no need for anyone to come in here since then, what with everyone out and about doing various jobs. Unease crept up his spine, a prickling sensation that brought on an involuntary shiver.

Someone had been in here without his permission.

Something was off, but he couldn't place it.

He walked towards the nearest desk, bobbing his head as though to confirm the suspicions swirling through his mind.

He booted up the main computer, pleased with his foresight in having them all linked. If anyone used one, he'd know. To the outsider, the computer appeared as it should. They wouldn't know he was able to access a programme that showed him every time someone logged on and what they did.

An icon on the lower toolbar shouted the fact a computer had been used since his check yesterday morning.

Interesting.

He hoped to find that someone had just fancied a game of solitaire before bed.

However, his gut told him otherwise.

Clicking an icon, he waited for the window to open and reveal the secrets it harboured. He stared at the information, incensed beyond measure. Anger boiled inside him at the audacity of whoever had breached the punters' files.

A fucking mole in my house. Who the hell is it?

Denzell immediately came to mind, him being the newest employee.

No, these files were accessed in the daytime when Denzell wasn't here. When only Gerry and Dave were here minding Stephen.

A blinding pain speared Cricket's head.

Stephen?

Surely not. And what about Gerry and Dave's report? Stephen had slept most of the day, only rising to make them some food, going back to his room just as the other employees had arrived home.

Either Gerry or Dave then.

Fucking wankers.

Seeing that one of them—or even both, working together—had tried to erase their history angered him further. What had they done with the information? Was it now in the hands of the police? Shit, he'd have to warn the punters, get rid of the damn lads.

So much to do in so little time.

Cricket switched on the ability to access the internet, opened Chrome, then his email account. Attaching the files, he sent them to James Klein, the man who ran the Spanish end of his business. He sighed. Everything would still be on the hard drive, but the information would be useless to anyone who tried to read it by the time he'd finished. He clicked the encrypt icon and imagined all those names and addresses changing into symbols. If the police got hold of these files now, it would take a fucking genius to work out what they held. Thankfully, whoever had used the computer hadn't sent any files via email.

He erased his history then shut the computer down. Reached into the desk drawer for a set of keys. He'd never had to lock the office before, but now it seemed he had to. Until the culprit was caught, that door would keep everyone out.

His face heated, the burn of rage creating the need for him to scratch his cheeks. Cricket left the room. He locked the door with a jerky flick of his wrist then stormed down the corridor to the other landing. Once there, he took in a steadying breath and lunged towards Gerry's bedroom door. The room was empty. He tried Dave's and found it the same way, so sped down the stairs, searching out his two employees with murder on his mind.

They sat with the others at the breakfast bar, plates of bacon and eggs in front of them. The steam of tea or coffee spiralled from their cups, and Cricket wanted to pick them up and dash the hot liquid in their faces.

"Which one of you two went into my office yesterday?" he demanded, chest tightening.

Gerry and Dave turned in their seats to look at him, faces a picture of confusion. They glanced at one another, some unspoken query bristling between them, then Gerry nodded.

Dave spoke up. "Neither of us. We were playing cards in the living room for most of the day— sorry, boss, I know that's not allowed. Like we said, Stephen was asleep." He frowned slightly, head cocking a bit. "Come to think of it, there *was* a noise up there at one point. You remember that, Gerry?" He stared at his friend.

Gerry palmed his chin. "Fuck me, yeah. Like someone squealed. I went up there to check it out, but no one was there. Stephen was still asleep."

Cricket's mind worked overtime. Either they were lying, or someone else had been in the house. Fucked off that the two men hadn't been manning the doors as he'd instructed, he said, "So someone got in. If you'd been doing your fucking *jobs*..." He spun away from them, clenching his fists and gritting his teeth. "Christ! You have no fucking idea what I just found. What could happen to *all* of us if... *Shit*."

He left the kitchen, sensing the shocked stares of his men on his back. He skidded on the tile. Upstairs, he lumbered towards Stephen's door, smashing it open so the handle bashed into the wall. A dull jingle of broken plaster showered the wooden floor.

Stephen sprang up in bed, his hair mussed, eyes wide. The rosy hue of sleep drained from his

156

cheeks, leaving him white, purple bags under his eyes standing out starkly. Even his lips paled above a quivering chin.

Cricket stared at him, not wanting to believe this beautiful trophy had `deceived him, but Stephen's expression said it all. The man clearly wasn't used to lying, hiding his emotions, and they played out now, his eyes flicking left to right, fingers whittling the quilt.

Why did it have to be you? I wanted... I had such good plans for us.

He put a stop to the musings of his heart. His mind had to take control now. Gerry and Dave had been relaxed, *normal*—no way could it have been them. Cricket had an inbuilt bullshit detector, one that had stood him in good stead over the years, and he smelt the stink of manure clear and strong.

And if it wasn't Stephen, then I need to find out who the fuck broke in and retrieved the information without Gerry and Dave knowing.

It wasn't possible, he knew that deep down, but his heart wanted another scenario. God, how his heart wanted that.

Focus.

"What the fuck were you doing in my office yesterday?" Cricket's temples throbbed with the pressure of his shout.

Stephen's mouth opened and closed several times, no sound emerging, and Cricket's anger grew to a higher level. No matter how much he'd wanted to share his life with this man, he wasn't about to let the little shit ruin everything he'd worked for. If Cricket's fast-beating heart was anything to go by, he'd have a fucking heart attack in a minute, and he wasn't having *that* either.

"Well?" he roared. "Cat got your bastard tongue?"

Murder again filled Cricket's mind.

"You accessed my files. What did you do with them?"

"N-n-nothing."

Stephen's response convinced Cricket he was telling the truth—no information had left this house, and the sale could go ahead.

"Get out of the fucking bed," he shouted, eyes wide, a headache forming at the back of his skull.

Stephen sat in shock.

Cricket saw red. "Disobey me, you bloody shit, and you'll know all about it. *Get out!*"

He grabbed Stephen's arm. Dragged him from the bed. Marched him naked to the stairs, breaths coming out of him in harsh bursts. Stephen cried, his attempts to pull away thwarted by Cricket gripping him harder. Giving him a shake at the top of the stairs, Cricket stopped himself from throwing him down them. Instead, he guided him to the foyer, fighting every step of the way to keep Stephen from unbalancing him. In the kitchen, he propelled him towards Jonathan, who'd turned in his seat at the breakfast bar to see what the commotion was.

"Something wrong, boss?" Jonathan asked, genuine concern on his face. He lowered his cup to the bar then balled his fists in his lap.

"Too fucking right there's something wrong." Cricket snorted out a breath through his nostrils.

"Please..." Stephen sobbed and stared at all the men.

They eyed him like he was shit on their shoes.

"Please, I didn't mean... I just wanted... I thought—"

Cricket sucked in a deep breath. "Shut the fuck *up*, you little *bastard*." He dug his fingers deeper into his flesh, hoping he caused as much pain as he was feeling.

Stephen cried out, bringing his free hand up to prise Cricket's fingers from his arm. Cricket dug deeper still and stared into Stephen's eyes. The man closed his mouth, snot dribbling from his nose, and barked out another harsh sob.

Why did you do it, eh? Now look what you've made me do.

"What needs doing, boss?" Jonathan stood and brushed toast crumbs from his suit.

"You'll need to get changed." Cricket eyed Jonathan up and down. He turned to Kevin. "And you. This one needs taking to the forest."

CHAPTER NINETEEN

Stephen was shunted along the white corridor by one of Cricket's men, his feet scuffing on the carpet. His mind whirled. How had Cricket found out? He'd erased everything he'd done on that computer.

He was dragged towards the mahogany door at the end, and he tried to think if he'd left anything out of place in the office. Maybe the computers hadn't been what had alerted Cricket to him being there yesterday. Maybe he'd mumbled in his dreams? He recalled, after Cricket had used him last night, falling asleep with that awful man holding him in a bear's embrace. Tight and unforgiving, a hug of ownership, possession. Despite trying to stay awake until Cricket had left the bed, Stephen had given up the fight and welcomed oblivion.

What if he'd been so tired he *had* mumbled about what he'd done?

No, Cricket would have woken him, surely. From the anger the man had displayed just now, there was no way he'd be able to hold that kind of rage in if he knew what Stephen had done before today.

Unless Redhead and Stocky *had* known what he'd been doing and had told Cricket this morning. But he didn't believe that. They'd have reported back to Cricket before bed last night, wouldn't they?

So how had Cricket found out?

It didn't matter now, did it. He was being taken down to the cellar. And what they would do to him at the forest didn't bear thinking about. If they needed to get changed, it meant they might get dirty...

One of Cricket's men unlocked the cellar door, and a chill sped through Stephen at the thought of going back down there. Would he be given more lemonade? Was this man going to force it down his throat in order to get the truth from him? There would be no point in that. It was obvious Stephen was the culprit. Why did Cricket need it confirmed?

His bladder throbbed with his desperation to use the loo. He clenched his teeth to ward off the pain and allowed the man to guide him down the dark steps. At the bottom, a light flicked on, the one above the metal central ceiling beam.

Oh God. Those chains.

His bladder shrieked.

Shuffles came from a far corner, and Stephen tensed.

He was pushed towards the hanging chains. Manacles were secured around his wrists. Cricket's man looked mean as hell, glaring at Stephen with black eyes filled with hate. His brown hair, slicked back in a low ponytail, emphasised his receding hairline. A pointed nose and eyes that were too close together reminded Stephen of a ferret.

"You should have just been his bitch." The man shook his head. "No good comes from crossing Cricket. Ah, well, you're fucked now all right."

He retreated to the stairs, and Stephen lost sight of him in the darkness. A clank sounded, and the chains tautened, lifting him off the floor. With his arms stretched above his head, he winced, the manacles digging into his wrists.

"You won't be hanging there long, I dare say," the man said, voice disembodied. "Won't be a minute before the other two have changed clothes, and they'll come back down for you. Still, best to make sure you can't escape, eh?" He laughed. "I won't be seeing you again. Let's just hope it's quick and painless, eh?"

The light went off, and his footsteps echoed up the stairs.

They're going to kill me. Oh shit, they're going to kill me. What about Mum? This is going to break her. Please, let me go home.

The door to the corridor closed, and a key twisted in the lock. Stephen relaxed his muscles—if he bunched them, it'd be more painful. He shook from head to foot, great racking jolts that jangled the chains, and he lost control of his bladder.

The sound of piss slapping the floor was loud in the darkness, and despite him being alone, shame heated his cheeks.

He said quick and painless.

What were they going to do? How were they going to kill him?

He entertained various death scenarios. None of them were any way to die, but he'd prefer a shot to the head any day. The quicker they killed him the better.

"Who's there?" came a voice.

Stephen cried out in alarm.

Oh fuck. Someone else is down here?

He sobbed.

A terrible thought struck him, snot dribbling over his lips and down his chin.

What if they go and get my brother next? What if they hurt Mum now because of what I did?

He released a long wail. All he could do now was pray Cricket would leave them alone.

"Hey," the voice said. "What's your name?"

"Stephen Hill," he said.

"What are you down here for?"

"Doesn't matter. Nothing does."

"Are they going to...kill you?"

"Yes."

"Where do you live? Can we get a message to anyone somehow?"

"You can't."

"Shit. There must be a way."

"If you get out of here," Stephen droned, "there's an office upstairs on the first floor. Internet access, but I don't know how to switch that on. And there are no phones anywhere. There's information on the computer."

"Okay. So where do you live?"

"Dowey Avenue. Fifty-four."

"All right, man. Anything you want us to say?"

Stephen pondered that for a minute. What *could* he say? "Just tell my mum...thanks for my life. And I'm sorry."

The door to the cellar creaked. Jonathan appeared at the edge of the circle of light, his gaze fixed on the floor. He sighed and raised a hand. A clang echoed, and Stephen lowered to the floor. He held out his hands for Jonathan to remove the manacles, allowed himself to be led towards the stairs.

The lights snapped off, and the man from the corner called, "We'll tell her."

Stephen's eyes stung. There was no point in crying, no point in hoping he wouldn't be taken to the forest. The only hope he had was that the man back there would manage to keep his word.

He trudged up the steps, knowing what condemned really meant, then walked down the white corridor, head bent and shoulders slumped. In the kitchen, he sensed the stares of the other men, the malice coming off them, and shrugged it off.

Jonathan urged him out into the foyer then through a doorway Stephen hadn't noticed before. They walked down another hallway, a windowed door to the outside world at the end. At one time he'd have been ecstatic to see it, the blue sky bright through the glass, the sun high. The sight chilled him now, and once at the door, he bowed his head so he wouldn't have to look at what he'd never see again.

Outside, Jonathan and Kevin flanked him, their grip tight on his upper arms. Stephen stumbled over the grass, the pointy blades tickling the soles of his feet, and remembered how it had felt as a child when Mum had chased him around the garden with the hose that long-ago summer day. His brother had been a baby, sitting in his pram and squealing, chubby hands clapping.

The memory hurt his chest.

The forest arrived in front of him in no time. Guided through the trees, the mulch and fallen leaves squelching between his toes, he entertained the past. A thousand and one treasured memories sped through his mind. He smiled, laughed at one point, uncaring whether the two men thought him mental. He'd had it good and didn't regret one minute of his childhood. The regrets he *did* have, well, they were in fate's hands now, and only she could keep Stephen's mum and brother safe.

A clearing appeared, an ominous mound of loose mud to his right. Someone else had been brought here recently then. He winced. Soon Stephen would join whoever it was in the cold, dark earth.

The men drew him to a stop at the far edge of the circular clearing. They released his arms and stepped back a few paces. Jonathan reached into his jacket. Pulled out a gun. Stephen was grateful for that. Even if they messed with his mind, shooting him in places where it would take hours for him to bleed to death, at least he'd know that by the time the sun set he'd be gone.

Jonathan raised the gun level with Stephen's head.

And pulled the trigger.

CHAPTER TWENTY

Cricket stared out of the office window, the best place in the house to see into the clearing. The gunshot startled him, even though he'd expected it. Stephen's body sagged to the ground. Birds cawed and flew from the trees, a murder of crows. Stephen sprawled there, legs bent at the knees, arms splayed out by his sides, so much whiteness against the green grass. Cricket recalled how that body had felt against him, and a tear trickled down his cheek. Hot. A sign of weakness.

He swiped it away and continued to observe.

Kevin strode over to the small shed at the back of the clearing and brought out two shovels. His two men worked tirelessly, digging the grave that would hold the man Cricket had had such high hopes for. He thought of Briggs and chuffed out a wry laugh that he could have done with him in the clearing now, what with him used to digging graves.

Cricket's eyes glazed as though gauze covered them. He thought about what he should do with those two in the cellar. Their firm friendship had struck him somewhere deep inside, and despite what his intentions had been when he'd ordered Denzell to go and fetch them, he couldn't bring himself to order them killed. Besides, Jonathan and Kevin had their work cut out for them already today. They wouldn't relish digging two more holes.

Having Briggs and Banks working for him seemed the best bet.

A couple of hours passed, the sun rising higher, clouds coming and going, their shapes changing while they chugged across the sky. Once Stephen had been lowered into that hole and the first shovels of dirt had been thrown in on top of him, Cricket left the window. He still needed to speak to his men, remind them of their duties, and he wanted to ensure Denzell understood when to open the gates for the security team and the punters.

Weary and out of sorts, he went into Stephen's room. Sat on the bed and fisted the quilt, bringing it up to his nose. He inhaled deeply, remembering how the scent had smelt fresh from Stephen.

I didn't get to read him a bedtime story.

With one last sigh, he told himself to move on. Leaving the room, he made his way downstairs to the kitchen. Everyone waited for him, and he barked out instructions. They nodded, not one of them rolling their eyes at his need to continually repeat instructions.

A loyal lot, his men.

CHAPTER TWENTY-ONE

Denzell entered Isaac's room. Guilt stabbed him for rushing the others with their breakfast this morning, and after their afternoon snack he'd urged them to hurry in the shower. He'd had to explain to them that they'd be leaving tonight and what was expected of them when they were taken to the waiting room prior to the viewing. Some had cried, others had looked at him with a vacant stare, and his heart had broken for every one of them. He'd bitten his tongue, holding back the words that hopefully the police would rescue them later, and once they were checked by the doctor and interviewed, they'd get to see their parents.

If they had any who gave a shit.

Isaac faced the wall again, this time beneath the covers. Denzell placed the tray holding a sandwich and a glass of milk on the chest of drawers then locked the door. Last night, when he'd texted Fairbrother, the detective had replied with a message that so long as Denzell let the 'security' men through the gate tonight, everything was in place on his end. Denzell had sighed with relief that the past six months had been worth all the effort.

"Isaac? I've brought you some food. Sorry it's just a sandwich again." He'd toyed with giving Isaac too much so his belly expanded. The punters wouldn't want him then. If things went wrong and Isaac ended up staying here for another six months, it would give Denzell time to work out how to get his brother out of there before the next auction.

What could go wrong, though?

Cricket could catch on that the security guards are coppers and shoot the fucking lot of them, that's what could go wrong.

But Fairbrother had the whole police force behind him, and it wouldn't be long before more officers showed up if Fairbrother didn't radio in with an update.

I'm panicking, that's all. One way or another, this stops tonight.

Isaac turned. He sat up and rubbed his eyes, his hair unkempt from where he'd slept. He'd been chatty this morning, and it seemed like he would be again now.

"I dreamed about my brother."

"You did? That's great. And what was the dream about?" Denzell took the tray over to the bed. He placed it on Isaac's knees.

"That I found him. He left a long time ago, see, and when *I* left, I looked for him all the time. Didn't see him, though."

Denzell's throat swelled. "Oh, right."

Isaac picked up one half of his sandwich— sliced chicken breast with mayonnaise. "Reckon I didn't find him because I wouldn't really know what he looks like now. He'd be different these days."

Swallowing the lump in his throat, Denzell turned away. Hands dangling between his open knees, he toyed with his fingers, something to focus on other than the tears burning his eyes.

"What d'you reckon he'd be like now then?" Denzell asked.

"That's easy," Isaac mumbled around the food. "He'd be like you."

"Ah. Poor bastard."

Isaac laughed, and Denzell chuckled, gazing at him. The smile in Isaac's eyes lightened his heart. Should he tell him who he was? He obviously didn't recognise him because of the thick beard.

175

I can't. He might blab. And if Cricket finds out I know this is my brother...

He shivered at the thought and faced away from Isaac to glare at the carpet. "So you ran away then?" he asked, wanting to make conversation.

"Yeah."

"How come?" *You know why.*

"Just...because."

"Same with me, mate."

"Why did you leave home?"

The milk glass rose in Denzell's peripheral vision. "Long story. Mum was a drug dealer, my dad was an alcoholic, and my grandad..." He'd said too much. Knew it as soon as the words had left his mouth.

"Hey! That's the same... That's shitty, that is. Where did you go?"

"Where everyone else goes. The city. Blended in with the other kids and older tramps."

"How did you manage to eat? I took food out of the bins, and on good days, after I'd pickpocketed and shit like that, I got food from McDonald's or Burger King. Or the hot dog van on Trident Square. He's nice, the bloke who runs it. Gives me extra meat on my kebabs. Says I need fattening up."

Isaac's words echoed in Denzell's mind. '*I took food out of the bins.*'

Shit, I didn't need to hear that.

"I managed same as you." Denzell was unwilling to let his brother know the horrors he'd been through to make money. He was just thankful Isaac hadn't had to do the same.

176

"It was all right." Isaac lowered the glass to the tray. He picked up the second half of his sandwich. "There was this old bloke, Pete his name was. He looked after me most nights."

Denzell snapped his head up in alarm. "He didn't—"

"No! No, nothing like that. He was like my grandad. Just a nice old man. Told me that the black van would get me, though."

"Did he?" Denzell's heart beat faster.

"Yeah, said it would come for me, and he was right."

"So, the van...Pete saw it often, did he?"

"Fuck, yeah. He's been on the streets a *long* time. Reckons that van's been coming for years. I saw it once. Some bloke got out of it, and he stared at me. Old Pete said they'd get me sooner or later, and here I am, in this fucking room." He sighed and put his sandwich back on the plate. "But it's all right. Pete will tell them I've gone."

"Them?"

"Yeah, the police. He said if he told them my name, they'd look for me."

"Oh, right."

Isaac stared at Denzell wide-eyed. "You won't... I mean, you won't tell that other man what I just said, will you?"

Denzell shook his head and smiled. "No, I won't tell him."

"Thanks."

"Right, I have to take you down into the cellar now."

Isaac's eyes widened further.

Denzell quickly added, "It's all right. I just have to get you showered, that's all. Tonight..." *No, I can't tell him the truth. Just give him the tale you gave the others.* "Tonight you'll be taken out of here. To a room with nine other lads. Some...people will be coming to take a look at you, but you won't see them."

Isaac frowned, his face paling. "What do they want to look at me for?"

Denzell cleared his throat. "Uh, they want to offer you a new home."

"Oh, right." Isaac's shoulders relaxed. "Is this like some kind of homeless adoption place or something?"

"Yeah, something like that."

"These people. Are they nice?"

"I don't know them." He was entering dangerous territory so stood, the horrible thought in his mind of whether Cricket had had enough time to sample Isaac prior to the sale. "When you're in The Viewing Room, you need to face the mirror on the wall, and when you're asked to turn around, or smile, or whatever they ask of you, do it."

"So they'll be inspecting me. Seeing if I'm what they want?"

"Yeah, that's right. Come on. Shower time."

Denzell held out his hand, but Isaac didn't take it. Knowing he had to maintain an air of authority and hating it, Denzell grasped Isaac's wrist and led him to the door. He took him down to the cellar, letting him shower for longer than he should have.

Briggs and Oliver remained silent in the corner on the mattress, but with the strip lights on, they'd have seen him bring every single boy down here today. If Briggs and Oliver weren't dead by the time the police arrived, they'd give statements. Denzell was in deep shit if they spilled everything as they saw it. Still, he hadn't touched any of the lads inappropriately, and that stood for something, surely? And Fairbrother knew he'd been working as an insider.

It'll be all right either way. If I get put inside, so be it. If I don't get put away? I'll find somewhere to live with Isaac.

He hadn't spent a penny of his earnings from here. He'd felt sick getting it, didn't want anything to do with dirty money, but if it meant setting him and his brother up in a flat, then he'd use it.

They were owed that much.

Isaac dried himself then covered his privates with cupped hands. Denzell wished he could give him something to wear. He took him upstairs and back to his room. If Denzell didn't return to the main house soon, Cricket would wonder what the fuck was going on. He couldn't afford the boss getting suspicious. Reticent to leave Isaac, he closed off his heart and used his head.

"I might see you later." He turned in the doorway to look at him.

"Yeah? All right then. You reckon someone might want me?"

"I don't know, mate." He smiled and lifted the tray. Once he'd left the room, he locked the door and muttered, "I fucking hope not."

CHAPTER TWENTY-TWO

Much later, Denzell stared through the living room window. Darkness had come down, cloaking the front grounds so the grass disappeared and the driveway resembled a faint beige strip. Clouds swept across the sickle moon, the stars barely discernible in the murk. He pressed a button on the keypad, and the Victorian lamps outside burst into life. Their glow wasn't enough to illuminate much beyond a few metres, but the security team waited out there on the main road, headlights switched off, engines silent.

He glanced at his watch. Cricket entered the room, and Denzell looked up at the boss, who appeared haggard, as though Stephen's murder played on his mind. For the first time, Denzell saw Cricket as a man with feelings and not just a wanker out to make money off the backs of young men.

Don't think of him like that. He's a bastard. Deserves what's coming to him.

"All right, boss?" He stared back out of the window.

"Five minutes, Denzell, then let the team in."

"Yep."

"Once security is in place, the punters will arrive. I know I've been through this with you before, but I want everything going right. So, like I said, once you open the gates, go out there and instruct the men as to where they need to be. Pick two for checking in the punters—the clipboard's in the foyer on the sideboard, and tell them to watch the crystal ornaments, for fuck's sake. Ten need to be in a line guarding the front of the house, and the rest should be dispersed around the back. Tell them if anything's off, shoot on sight, unless they recognise one of us or the punters. A shot to the kneecap is preferable, just in case it's someone who shouldn't have been gunned." Cricket sighed as if his speech had been a trial.

Denzell eyed the boss, nodding, facing the window again.

"When the auction's over," Cricket said, "and the punters have gone with their purchases, security need to do a sweep of the property to make sure no one's been left behind. I trust no fucker, so this part of the plan is important. Parker once had some trouble—a customer had brought someone with him without signing him in. Found the nonce in the house, searching for a lad. Didn't fancy buying one, did he, thought he could just take." He snorted. "I'm not fucking having *that* happen again." He clamped a hand on Denzell's shoulder and squeezed. "You got all that?"

"Yep, boss. Don't worry, I'm on it." Denzell smiled.

"Good man. Oh, and those two down in the cellar. Get them cleaned up. Suited nicely—you know where the spare clothes are. I want them in The Viewing Room with me. Been thinking of taking them on, know what I mean?"

"Good idea."

Cricket chuckled. "The fates smiled on me when they sent you my way."

He stalked out of the room, and Denzell blew out a huge breath.

He stared through the window again. Headlights pierced the darkness out on the road. Pressing the button that opened the gates, he waited until the convoy of five black Jeeps eased along the track then up the driveway. He collected the clipboard from the foyer and left the house, nodding to Jonathan, who guarded the door from inside.

At the head of the drive, he pointed the drivers to his right, waving to tell them they should go around the side of the mansion and park on the large square of asphalt. The last car turned, and he followed. By the time he reached the car park, the twenty 'security' men stood together behind one car.

Denzell approached Fairbrother, the detective dressed identical to the other men—black combat trousers, bomber jackets, and baseball caps. Jerking his head so Fairbrother followed, Denzell led him to the edge of the car park and relayed everything Cricket had told him. He gave him the clipboard.

Fairbrother nodded. "Text just before the customers get ready to leave, when everyone is still in The Viewing Room. *Before* the lads are taken."

"Yeah." Denzell glanced around nervously, hoping Cricket hadn't planted one of his men out here in the darkness.

"Good." Fairbrother patted Denzell's shoulder. "I'd rather my men storm the house when the lads are still safe." He paused, then, "I'm sorry about your brother being here."

"Yeah, well...he'll be all right in an hour or two, won't he?"

"He will."

"If...if I'm nicked, make sure Isaac isn't returned home. Mum and Dad, they—"

"I know." He paused once more. "I'll brief my men now then." Fairbrother patted Denzell again.

"Right. See you later." Denzell moved to walk away, then remembered he'd forgotten to tell Fairbrother something. "Oh, the young man, Stephen?"

"Yes?"

"He was shot today."

"Fuck!" Fairbrother sighed.

"Buried with the other lad who hanged himself. Down the bottom of the garden. There's some trees."

"Right."

Denzell headed for the house. The darkness spooked him, seeming to close in on him, an unwelcome hug. He hurried towards the Victorian lamps, thankful for their brightness as he strode along the front of the house. He reached the steps by the black doors, and footsteps crunched behind him. He glanced back. Two officers walked to the gates and another two approached the front steps.

This is it then. No turning back now.

He entered the house. In the living room, he jabbed his thumb on the button to close the gates for now. It wouldn't be long and the punters would arrive, a caterpillar of cars wheeling along the drive, containing some of the sickest people on Earth. Denzell gritted his teeth, angry that so many of these nights had gone before—and he hadn't known anything about them.

Where are those young men now? Some are fucked-up in the head, no doubt—if they're alive.

He couldn't lose concentration. Had to focus on the here and now.

A shuffle of feet rustled out in the foyer, and he turned from the window to gaze through the living room doorway. Cricket's men paraded past, each holding a lad by the wrist.

Poor bastards.

Reminding himself it would all be over soon, he waited for sight of Isaac. He came last in the line, and as if his brother sensed Denzell's stare, Isaac glanced through the doorway and nodded in acknowledgement, holding one hand up, fingers crossed.

Christ, he really thinks he's being adopted.

The pain of Denzell's throat swelling had him turning away, and he etched that last image of Isaac into his mind in case he never saw him again.

Focus! Focus on the fucking job.

A convoy of cars drove down the main road on the other side of the iron-railed fence. He prodded the gate button and waited until the last of the vehicles had swerved right and headed towards the car park. He closed the gates then the curtains, shutting out the sight of a copper's back outside the window.

Once Denzell had texted Fairbrother with the go-ahead, it was down to the detective from there on out. What came after could turn nasty, what with the police and Cricket's men being armed.

He stood in the middle of the room and patted his gun, tucked snugly in his waistband.

Hoped he never had to use it.

With a deep breath, he left the living room, purposely keeping his gaze away from where the young men had been taken. Upstairs, he selected a couple of suits, two shirts, ties, underwear, socks, and shoes. He also grabbed fresh towels and a new bottle of shower gel. He took everything down to the cellar.

He flicked on the light. Someone cursed. It was too bright then. He hung the clothes on a hook and placed the towels and gel on a chair beside the shower stall.

He walked towards the two men on the mattress.

One was awake, the other appeared to be asleep.

"Right," he said. "You've got yourself a reprieve."

CHAPTER TWENTY-THREE

Langham sat up and stared at Beardy. Had he heard him right? "What do you mean?"

"Cricket wants you upstairs tonight."

"What for?" He eyed the man with suspicion.

Beardy dug into his pocket for a bunch of keys and stood on the mattress, feet either side of Langham's thighs. "If you try anything when I unlock you, just bear in mind every man upstairs is armed. So am I. And if I have to shoot you, I will. I won't want to, but, if needs must..." He slid the key into the manacle.

Langham cringed, lifting his free, heavy arm. He dropped it to the mattress, the chain's jingle sending a rush of apprehension up his spine. A reprieve sounded good in one way but ominous in another. Wasn't Cricket just delaying the inevitable?

"You didn't answer my question," Langham said. "What are we going upstairs for?"

Beardy gave Langham a sideways glance. "Look, I *could* tell you there's nothing to worry about. I *could* tell you that after you've gone upstairs and seen whatever it is Cricket wants you to see, heard whatever it is Cricket has to say, everything will be all right. But I won't have told you anything. D'you understand what I'm saying?"

Did he? He thought so, but he didn't dare hope.

"So, you're telling me we ought to just do as we're told and everything will be fine," Langham said.

Beardy inserted the key into Oliver's manacle. "Yeah, that's what I'm saying. It might not seem like that when you're up there, but trust me, things'll pan out. I didn't say a word. I never told you anything, got it?" He eased the manacle off Oliver's wrist, gently, with *care*.

What the fuck? He's acting like he gives a shit.

"Trust you?" A tired laugh left Langham's parched mouth. "Listen to yourself, will you? Trust you, my arse. Would *you* trust you if you were me? I don't think so."

Beardy stared. "Listen, let him sleep for a bit longer, yeah? You need to shower, get yourself ready."

Langham looked down at his wrists, rings of red, bruises a fierce purple backdrop to the rivers of blue veins showing prominently through his skin.

"I need to shower? What, doesn't Cricket like killing dirty people?" He chuckled at his joke, getting up on all fours and dragging himself to the end of the mattress. He winced, aches and pains taking over his body.

"Fuck." Beardy sighed and rasped a hand over that black beard. He looked up at the ceiling as if asking for guidance, then back down again, pinning Langham with his gaze. "If I tell you something, you need to keep it to yourself."

Langham nodded. *What's going on?* He tried to stand but failed.

"Stay put for a minute," Beardy said. "And give him a nudge, will you?" He jerked his thumb towards Oliver. "I've changed my mind about him sleeping. He needs to hear this, too."

Langham studied Beardy for a minute. His instincts told him to trust the bloke, and he reasoned that was all he had left now, instincts. Maybe having everything stripped away—dignity, life as he knew it—left him with only the base tools he needed to survive.

He leant back and shook Oliver's shoulder. "Wake up."

Oliver shifted, pain scrunching his face even in sleep.

"Come on. You've got to wake up."

Oliver opened his eyes, blinking in the light. He groaned, raising one hand to shield his eyes. "What's going on?"

"The big bastard who took us is here." Langham gave Beardy an apologetic glance.

"My name's Denzell," Beardy said. "Just so you know. I'll wait over here until you're showered before I tell you what I have to say, but try and get a move on, yeah?" He checked his watch.

Langham regarded him for a moment. Something about—Denzell, did he say?—told him the man wasn't acting like someone loyal to his boss. Him telling Langham everything would be all right wasn't consistent with what he knew of him prior to now. What was his game?

He's fucking going against Cricket? Jesus Christ...

"What's going on?" Oliver repeated. He eased up onto his elbows, face creasing once again, a gasp and curse leaving him.

"I'm not sure." Langham looked over his shoulder. "But we need to get showered and dressed. And Denzell has got something to tell us. Reckons it's going to be all right when we go upstairs."

Oliver shifted to sit beside him. "All right? What the fuck is all right about this place? And does all right mean not dead? Fuck, this shit is doing my head in."

"All right means not dead," Denzell said. "All right means going home."

Langham snapped his head forward, staring at Denzell. "Look, stop fucking with us. I'm too tired for this bullshit."

Denzell pushed off the wall then strode towards them, face lighting up, animated, as though he had new purpose. "I reckon I can trust you, so—"

Langham's laugh cut him off. "That's rich! Bloody hell, you're something else, you are."

Denzell hunkered down before them, hands dangling between his splayed legs. "I know what this looks like, but I'm not what or who you think I am."

"And what's that? You're not a fucking nutcase?" Langham asked.

Oliver coughed. "Hear the bloke out. We've got nothing to lose at this point. We could be dead either way..." He shrugged.

Langham turned back to Denzell. "Okay. Give us what you've got."

As Denzell whispered what he'd been doing for the past six months, admiration for him grew inside Langham, despite telling himself this could all be some elaborate trick. What a turnabout if Denzell was telling the truth. Langham had gone from distrusting him to respecting him, yet still a sliver of doubt writhed in his belly. This could be one massive mind-fuck, designed for them to let their guard down.

"Everything's going to plan so far." Denzell put his hands on his knees and pushed himself standing. "Fairbrother and his men are in place."

Fairbrother? Thank fuck for that...

Denzell peered back at the stairs, obviously worried they were being overheard. "Cricket's got it into his head you two will want to work for him. Now, this is where you have to play along. When he puts the suggestion to you—and really, if I hadn't told you this shit you'd have no choice but to agree if you want to live—try and react like you would if you didn't know what's going to happen. If he suspects... That's why I never said anything before. I had to play it carefully, make him think I was 'one of the boys'." His bottom lip trembled. "And believe me, at times it's been fucking hard."

Langham felt sorry for Denzell. He couldn't imagine doing something like that for six months. And that kid hanging himself—man, it was awful.

"Right." Langham slowly eased off the mattress. "Shower time."

Standing proved more difficult than he'd thought. His muscles protested at him using them so soon after they'd been damaged, and his skin, taut from the crusted blood around the welts, drew tighter. He took a tentative step. The promise of going home in a few hours gave him the determination to walk over to the shower.

Two fresh towels with a bottle of gel on top had never looked so normal, a signal that the terrible turn his and Oliver's lives had taken might be about to go in a different direction again—one that led to better things.

I need to trust Denzell. If he's lying, then... Don't think about that. Deal with that if it happens. Just trust him for now. How would he know Fairbrother if he wasn't telling the truth? Unless Fairbrother's in on it.

It was difficult to trust anyone, but he allowed hope to blossom inside him, relishing the warmth it gave his tired and hurting body. His mind became more alert, and he set the shower to warm, knowing anything hotter would have him screaming in pain. He glanced back at Oliver, who nodded. Denzell gave a wonky smile. Returning the grin, feeling better than he had even two minutes ago, Langham got under the spray.

He reached out to the chair, grabbing the bodywash. Was it wise to use soap? It would sting, but his cuts needed cleaning before they festered with infection.

The soap did sting.

Gritting his teeth, he carefully washed. He inspected his body. The welts didn't look so bad now they'd been cleaned up. The bruises were another matter. A blue, purple, and bright-pink map of the damn world covered his body. The towel against them brought fresh pain, and dressing was even worse. Material chafing on raw wounds wasn't something he savoured, but if it meant getting out of here, he'd endure it.

The shirt was a little too big, the suit trousers a little too long, but the jacket was roomy enough that he could move without the fabric rubbing much. He stepped into the shoes—a tad tight on the toes, but nothing compared to what he'd suffered so far—and he was less a prisoner, more a human being.

While Oliver showered, Langham spoke with Denzell, who elaborated some more.

"Like I said to Oliver when you were showering, Cricket had someone killed today."

"Shit. Who?"

"Young bloke called Stephen Hill."

Langham felt sick. "So this Fairbrother. You trust him?"

"Yeah. I should have let him in on everything right from the start, but I wanted the punters caught, too, you know?"

"Yeah, but Cricket's got to have information on the customers somewhere. No way would he not have kept a log of who they are. It's his insurance in case any of them grass him up."

"I heard he's got this hi-tech computer system." Denzell paused, frowning. "Saying that, Stephen accessed the information. That's why Cricket had him shot."

"Makes no sense. If the information was available, Fairbrother could have caught the punters that way. Look, I'm not saying what you did was wrong, but those kids could have been home with their parents *sooner*, know what I mean?"

Denzell nodded, his marred brow showing he wrestled with his conscience. "Yeah, I see what you're saying, but I wasn't allowed out of Cricket's sight until I picked you and Oliver up. There was nowhere I could buy a memory stick without being seen. I had my plan in place, didn't want to deviate from it. Reckoned if I did, everything would go wrong. It's done now, and we are where we are. I can't undo the past or fix that mistake now, and the lads...I made sure they were well cared for all the way. If I thought they'd be harmed after Cricket initiated them, I would've told Fairbrother where to come sooner."

Denzell was justifying his actions while dealing with a shitload of guilt over his decisions.

Langham nodded. "What's done is done. All we can hope for is everything works out so no innocents get hurt."

He glanced over to the shower stall. Oliver had stepped out and gingerly wrapped a towel around his body. Langham returned his attention to Denzell—he couldn't deal with watching Oliver in pain when he knew how bad that towel felt as it abraded the skin.

"Besides," Denzell said, "Cricket's been playing a game with me." He gave Langham a grim look, eyes moist, lips a thin straight line.

"By doing what?"

"You know I told you earlier one of the lads hanged himself?"

"Yeah."

"Well, Cricket had a replacement picked up. Reckon he's testing me, seeing if I'm loyal to him or not."

"What d'you mean? What's a new one got to do with it?"

"The newbie is my brother."

What the *hell* went through Cricket's mind? He was damn insane.

"Oh fuck. Jesus Christ." Langham blinked, digesting the information.

"Yeah, but I've made out I don't know Isaac's here. That's my brother, by the way. And Isaac doesn't know I'm his brother."

"How come?" Langham frowned harder.

"Because I left home years ago. Remember me telling you that? He was much younger, and I don't look the same anymore." Denzell tugged his beard. "I've talked to him about his brother, and fuck..." He bit his wobbling lip and took a deep breath through his nose. "He said he's been searching for me ever since he left home." His voice broke on the last word. "But that...but that he wouldn't know what I looked like now."

Langham rested a hand on Denzell's meaty forearm. "Listen, you've done the right thing. Isaac and the others are going to be all right now. Who knows, if the police can get the information off Cricket's computer, a shitload more young men will be all right, too. You've got to believe that. As for Cricket playing games with you... He's one fucked-up wanker who deserves everything he gets."

"Yeah. And the others. Jonathan and Kevin are the worst. They're the ones who abduct and kill people who piss Cricket off." Denzell straightened his shoulders, shaking his body out as though erasing all the kinks his confession had brought.

Oliver limped over, dressed now.

Denzell said, "Listen. I'm fucking sorry for putting you through this, yeah? But I had no choice. I had to get those lads free, and you two going through what you did... Small price to pay." He smiled sheepishly. "I know you won't feel that way—you're the ones who got the whipping—but those lads..."

Langham cleared his throat. "It's all right. We didn't enjoy it, but fuck, if it means those people going home, then I'd go through it all again."

And he meant every word.

CHAPTER TWENTY-FOUR

Oliver had never winced or cringed so much in his life. Now, with all that information swirling through his head, he struggled to make sense of it. Yeah, Denzell had explained it well enough. Oliver's mind was sluggish from whatever drugs he'd been given and from the lack of food and water. It refused to cooperate as it would if he'd been told these things before all...this.

Denzell led Oliver and Langham up the cellar stairs—every step weighty and achy—and Oliver thought about what lay ahead and shivered. Denzell unlocked the door then ushered them into the corridor. His head throbbed, the stronger light exacerbating the incessant ache, and he winced—again.

"Cricket will be in The Viewing Room. Or maybe the living room." Denzell locked the door.

Why did he do that when no one else was down there?

Force of habit?

Denzell paved the way down the corridor. "I don't know what he's going to say to you, what he expects you to do tonight, if anything, but I suspect he'll ask you to work for him." He let out a breath. "No, he'll *tell* you you're going to work for him. Just agree. Do whatever it takes to get you through the next couple of hours." At the end of the corridor, he slid a key into the lock then turned it. "From here on out, act like you would if I hadn't let you in on this shit. Don't even *look* at me if you can help it." He lifted his arms and plonked his bear-like hands down, one on each of their shoulders. "Good luck. And if I don't see you again after tonight...well, have a good one."

Swinging the door wide, he allowed Oliver and Langham through then secured the door behind them.

"This way." He took them through the massive kitchen.

202

Oliver glanced at Langham, who appeared nervous. Pinched features, blanched cheeks. His hands shook a bit.

"It'll be all right," Oliver whispered. Although spirit hadn't told him that, he had to believe it.

Langham nodded. Denzell guided them across the foyer and through a door to the right. Oliver stared at a massive two-way mirror that spanned the opposite wall, shocked by the sight of a bright spotlight casting a funnel of illumination inside the room beyond. Black surrounded that funnel, and a shudder rippled up Oliver's spine—he imagined the lads standing there being inspected.

An empty row of black, easy leather chairs, ten in all, stood in front of the mirror, ready to hold the arses of perverts and deviants in the guise of respectable businessmen. They even got to bid in comfort. Sickened, Oliver wanted to lash out at the man who stood directly behind those chairs, his wide back and height proclaiming him as someone not many would mess with.

The man turned to face them.

Cricket.

"Here they are, boss." Denzell nodded at Langham and Oliver. "Want me to go back to the living room window? Keep an eye out?"

"Yes, Denzell. Good man. Thank you." Cricket stared first at Langham, then Oliver.

Denzell left the room, and Oliver experienced a sense of loss, like their anchor had been pulled up, leaving them buoyant and vulnerable.

Cricket narrowed his dark eyes and tilted his head, regarding them in a silent stare. He studied Langham, who clenched his jaw and fists.

"Gentlemen," Cricket said. "I have a proposition for you."

Here we go.

Cricket laced his fingers down by his groin. He laughed, the sound strangely normal. But what had Oliver expected? Some maniacal jangle that proved this man was insane?

"Well," Cricket said. "Hardly a proposition. Let me try again. I have an *order* for you. You're now working for me." He grinned, perfect white teeth on display. "For tonight, you'll just observe the culmination of months' worth of hard graft. This is what you'll be helping us achieve again in six months." He lifted one arm, encompassing the room. "Watch and learn what hard work and determination can do. Of course, you won't be allowed to leave the house for a while yet—got to earn my trust—but I have a good feeling about you two." He nodded, patted them on their shoulders, then laced his hands again. "Reckon you could become the next Jonathan and Kevin. My two top men, by the way. Yes"—he nodded again, as though trying to convince himself he spoke the truth—"you'll do nicely. Get paid, too."

He laughed uproariously then, and Oliver managed to stop the *Fuck you!* on his tongue and a frown from forming.

"So, what do you reckon to that?" Cricket eyed them, clearly expecting nothing but their agreement.

"Doesn't much look like we have a choice, does it?" Langham said, his tone surly.

Cricket widened his eyes and rocked on his feet. "That's right, my old son, you don't." He smiled at Oliver. "He's a bright one, isn't he?"

"Yeah," Oliver said.

Cricket beamed. "And what about you, Banks? What's your take on this?"

"Better than fucking dying." Oliver forced a jovial conspirator's chuckle.

"Excellent. Fucking *knew* I'd read you right." Cricket seemed pleased with himself—too pleased. "In a short while, the punters will be shown into this room. You'll observe from the back here, beside the door. You'll understand what this is all about very soon. Any questions, save them for later. All you need to do is watch and shut the fuck up. Absorb." He led them to their places. "Mike here will keep you company for the time being. I'll be back shortly." He left via a door to the right of the mirror.

He's going to check on the lads, I'll bet. This is so fucking nasty I can't stand it. The way I feel now, I don't know how Denzell's managed to act the way he has for so long.

Oliver glanced at Langham, who stood to his left, and gave a supportive smile. Mike loomed in the corner, eyes facing forward, but Oliver sensed he watched them. Jesus, he was a big bloke, all muscle and brawn. His blond hair was shaved at the sides and back and cropped short on top. His body gave more weight to the term 'built like a brick shithouse'.

205

Fuck being on the end of his fist.

Oliver stared forward but caught in his peripheral vision another man coming in the doorway Cricket had disappeared through. Oliver shifted his gaze so it appeared he was staring above the man's head at the lintel. If the bloke looked his way, he wouldn't think he was being studied. The fella crossed his arms over his barrel chest and stood with legs apart. No bastard was getting past *him* without a fight.

A sharp knock startled Oliver, and the huge man turned to open the door behind him. A parade of suited men came in, of various ages. Ranging from mid-thirties to sixties, from many ethnicities, the men each took a seat. From where Oliver stood, he could just make out ten pairs of legs, all in assorted poses. Crossed at the knee. Crossed at the ankle. One ankle balanced on a knee.

Christ, it's like they're here for a fucking jolly get-together. No nerves showing in any of them.

They chatted between themselves about their excitement at purchasing a new 'toy'.

Cricket entered the room again. Oliver made his expression blank—at least he hoped it was blank—gaze focused on the cone of light behind the mirror.

"Gentlemen!" Cricket took up residence in front of them, nodding and smiling to some of the men. "Tonight is the night you've all been waiting for. As usual, if you lift the right arm of your chair, you'll find a keypad inside. When each item is brought into the room behind me—possibly *your* precious new plaything if you win—you may use the buttons there to bid. As you'll see, at the top of the keypad is a small screen, which will show you the starting price. As each one of you bids, the price will change. Of course, some of you may not bid on one particular morsel—he may not be to your liking, I understand that—but if you *do* bid, please note that once no one has continued to bid three minutes after the last, the auction for that particular bundle of arse is closed."

He grinned, getting right on Oliver's nerves.

Cricket went on. "Obviously, the highest bidder wins. You may bid for as many toys as you wish. As you're aware, as soon as your funds have reached my account tonight, you may take your prize home." He clapped once. "Any questions?"

No one spoke.

"Good. So, without further ado, let the bidding begin!" Cricket strode across the room towards the big crop-haired bloke, nodding for him to go through the door.

So the big bloke's the one who'll take the lads into that room then.

Around a minute later, the door to the room behind the mirror opened towards them, and a young man walked inside. Oliver's stomach contracted, and it took every ounce of strength he had not to rush over and get the 'toy' out.

The lad stood beneath the light, as he'd no doubt been instructed, and stared straight ahead. He'd probably be looking at his own reflection, as from what Denzell had told them earlier, he'd be thinking someone had come to offer him a new home.

It was difficult to remain stoic, uncaring, as though what was happening was normal. Nothing. All in a day's work.

A few of the men leant forward, and one, a wiry-bodied bald bloke with a goatee to compensate for his lack of hair, left his seat to press his face to the glass for a better glimpse. He returned to his chair then jabbed his keypad, earning quick glances from the other customers.

Customers. Christ, like they're just buying meat at the market.

And they were, if he were honest.

Oliver swallowed bile.

Cricket raised a walkie-talkie to his lips. "Turn around."

The lad did so, presenting his back to the window and gaining the men's full attention. His backside was, after all, their main concern.

Oh God...

Oliver wanted to look at Langham but didn't dare.

Visions of previous nights like this one filtered into Oliver's mind, and he had to fight to keep from thinking about what the young men went through once they left this house. Despite what Cricket had been doing all these years, at least the kids were well fed and cared for here, albeit left alone for the most part to become catatonic or crazy from loneliness and fear, from missing their families.

Langham's hitching breaths brought Oliver up short, and he glanced at him. Langham's lips shivered as he struggled to maintain composure.

Was it because he'd known this case should have been solved years ago when he'd been a PC? That if his senior officers had listened to him, this night and many others would never have happened?

This was too real, too shocking, too damn much. Oliver sucked in a breath and observed Cricket. The man was intent on studying the figure behind the glass.

"Turn to the side," he said.

The lad did as he'd been instructed, showing the room his slender profile. Passivity came off him. Where had he gone inside that head of his? Was he imagining himself back at home, safe with his parents? Or had he locked himself in a virtual room, where emotions didn't play a part and he was kept safe?

Another flurry of jabs at keypads, then a tense three minutes passed.

Cricket pulled a phone-like machine from his pocket and glanced at it. He looked up and beamed at the men. "Sold, to Mr Ainsworth, for the sum of two hundred thousand pounds!"

CHAPTER TWENTY-FIVE

Cricket loved this part of the process almost as much as he loved the beginning, when new young men were brought home. To see the culmination of the past six months coming to fruition was like nothing else.

The ninth one stood behind the mirror now, surly and nothing like how he'd been told to look—*if* Denzell had explained everything right. Cricket had expected as much from this young man. He was about nineteen, clearly knew why he was here and what tonight was about, even though Denzell had been instructed not to tell them. He didn't doubt Denzell. No, far from it. Number Nine had sense enough to put two and two together. After all, who the fuck locked men in rooms while they were naked and ordered them to turn around on demand?

This one had taken it upon himself to put the punters off, Cricket saw that as plain as day. It didn't matter. Mr Hawthorn there, the customer rubbing his cock through his trousers in full view of everyone, liked a bed partner with a bit of the *little bastard* about him. With his free hand, Hawthorn jabbed at the keypad, making it clear he expected to win the boy.

Hawthorn, a jowly fucker with bushy black eyebrows and a penchant for the booze, had been recommended by another punter. Cricket had checked him out, finding nothing untoward on paper or via his contacts. But upon meeting him for the first time, a couple of months ago now, Cricket had experienced a touch of the heebie-jeebies. This bloke, for all the world trying to make an impression on Cricket, hadn't quite made the *right* impression. Cricket didn't like a know-it-all, and Hawthorn knew it all in spades. Or so he seemed to think. He'd spoken over Cricket when he'd been explaining the process and hadn't been able to get to grips with having to wait for his new toy.

After thinking about Hawthorn for several days, the time away from the man had dulled Cricket's unease. Consoling himself with the fact his men were armed and wouldn't hesitate to take Hawthorn out if he caused trouble, Cricket had let the burly, overbearing man be accepted as a customer.

Cricket smiled now at Hawthorn's frantic prodding of the bid button. The man's hair, reminiscent of a brown scouring pad, bobbed with his movements, and Cricket turned away to fix his gaze on the cargo.

While the bidding proceeded, he recalled what had happened when Number Nine had first been brought here.

The boy sat on a wooden chair in the middle of the room, anger subdued. Two spots of high colour stood out on his cheeks, and he'd lost his Nike baseball cap since coming down here. Cricket would have to make sure it was found. Burnt.

"Hello," Cricket said, standing about a metre in front of him.

Some lads, despite the lemonade, struck out. Cricket didn't fancy a bruised shin.

"Fuck you," the kid slurred.

"Now, now. No need to be nasty."

"You're so fucking dead." He eyed Cricket with hate.

"Oh, really? I rather think it could be the other way around if you don't shut the fuck up and tell me what I want to know."

Cricket's tone had unsettled him.

The lad glanced down at the floor until another bout of defiance gripped him. "Even if you kill me, you're still dead."

"How so?" Cricket asked, curiosity piqued at the certainty in the little fucker's voice.

"My dad's a copper." He sneered.

"And that helps you how?" Cocky shit.

"He'll find me. Find you. Lock you up."

"Ah, but it's not as easy as that, is it? Consider this. What if no one saw you taken? What if no one saw the van?"

"Someone will have, you'll see."

Cricket smiled at the fact the lemonade appeared to be doing its job. No need for an injection with this one. "Right. If you say so."

"I do."

"So tell me." Cricket studied the blond hair, the undefined jaw, the angry blue eyes. "What's your father's name?"

"You don't need to know that," he said.

Cricket shrugged. Sampled him, proclaimed him suitable, then left him in Denzell's care.

Cricket stared at him now, smug in the knowledge he'd be going on to a life without his father in it. Six months hadn't changed this one. He still had the same fighting spirit he'd arrived with, and Hawthorn, who jabbed the keypad several more times, was possibly the only man Cricket knew who could tame him.

Cricket lifted the walkie-talkie. "Turn around and face the back wall."

The cargo stared at the mirror, defiance bleeding out of him. If he didn't turn within thirty seconds, Cricket would go in there and make sure he fucking did. He glanced at Hawthorn to check the man's reaction. The boy still hadn't turned, and a lecherous grin spread over the punter's face.

Cricket repeated his request.

The copper's son remained in place.

Cricket entered the corridor then shoved his man guarding the door to The Viewing Room out of the way. He took a deep breath to compose himself. Inside, shielded from view by the door, he growled, "Fucking turn around or your father'll find himself minus a damn son."

The cargo blinked several times and appeared to be weighing the truth in Cricket's statement. Whether his tone brooked no argument or the lad thought it best to just do as he'd been told, he faced the back wall.

"Good," Cricket said. "And when I ask you to turn and face *this* door, fucking do that, too." He barged out and stepped into The Viewing Room. "Sorry about that, gentlemen. It seems our little guest doesn't know how to behave."

Hawthorn's eyes gleamed. He got up to approach the window, observing the goods with wide eyes. Cricket analysed the other guests, those with seats beside Hawthorn appearing disgruntled that he blocked their view.

"If you could retake your seat, sir." Cricket took a step forward.

Hawthorn ignored him.

"Please, sir. The other guests can't see." Cricket stretched out a hand to place it on Hawthorn's arm.

Hawthorn threw it off. "This one's mine."

Cricket gave an unsteady laugh. "It doesn't quite work like that. You read the bidding rules. They apply to everyone."

"Get him out of the fucking way," another guest said. "And if he can't abide by the rules, get him the hell out."

Unused to such behaviour—Hawthorn *was* new, and shit, Cricket wished he'd vetted him better now—Cricket had to think on his feet. "Mr Hawthorn. Please return to your seat, otherwise my men will have to escort you off the property."

Hawthorn ignored him again.

Cricket sighed. "And they are armed."

While Hawthorn had been at the mirror, Cricket had noted from his peripheral vision the other men bidding fast and furiously. By the time Hawthorn returned to his chair, he'd find the price had risen dramatically.

Hawthorn reluctantly ripped his gaze from the lad to stare at Cricket. Lips wet and slack, he dashed his tongue out to lick them. "Like I said, that one's mine." He stomped back to his seat, flopping down then leaning towards his keypad. His eyes bulged at the amount on the screen.

Cricket peeked at his little machine.

The boy currently cost half a million pounds.

"This is fucking rigged!" Hawthorn shouted, leaping from his chair. "When I went up to that window, that kid cost a hundred grand."

Anticipating trouble—real trouble—Cricket gave Mike the nod.

"Sir." Cricket waved a placating hand. "If you'd just like to bid again..."

Hawthorn bunched his fists, standing in the middle of the room. Mike strode towards him, and Cricket caught a glimpse of Briggs and Oliver as they watched, their faces showing shock and more than a little concern.

Mike took hold of Hawthorn's arm. "Are you going to sit down?"

Hawthorn attempted to shake Mike off but failed.

"I repeat, for the last time I might add, are you going to sit down?" Mike glowered.

Cricket had a bad feeling about this.

Hawthorn raised his other arm. His fist connected with Mike's jaw, sending him sprawling backwards. The other customers rose as one, converging on Hawthorn to defuse the situation. Somehow, Hawthorn broke free of the scrum and headed directly for Cricket. Quickly opening the door and barking an order at his man in the hallway to secure the boys, Cricket then slammed the door and pressed his back against it, facing the madness in The Viewing Room.

Hawthorn reached him in a second, clamping his hands around Cricket's throat.

CHAPTER TWENTY-SIX

Sounds of a commotion spurred Denzell to the living room doorway. He stared across the foyer, just making out a lad standing in the spotlight, his back to the room. None of the customers sat in their chairs. Strangled groans filtered to him along with muffled shouts and curses.

What the fuck?

Briggs and Oliver appeared in the doorway, Oliver looking left then right, for somewhere to run, no doubt.

What the hell was going on? Had something gone wrong?

Denzell marched across the foyer, dipping his hand in his jacket for his mobile in order to text Fairbrother. It wasn't there.

Fuck!

He patted himself, panic taking over his limbs, his heartbeat accelerating and his pulse thudding in his ears. It would mean he'd have to alert Fairbrother to his face, and if Cricket saw him…

Denzell chanced a peek inside The Viewing Room. The punters surrounded Cricket, apparently trying to pull a man off him, whose hands held tight around Cricket's neck.

Go on, kill the son of a bitch.

Jonathan reached the melee at the same time as a staggering Mike. Guns would be drawn any second.

While the people in The Viewing Room were distracted, Denzell made a snap decision. Yanking open the front door, he glanced about for Fairbrother, who spun from his position at the bottom of the steps, his stance showing he was ready for action. Briggs and Oliver barged past Denzell and out into the night. Fairbrother stared at them.

"Wait!" Denzell said, breaths coming hard and fast. "These two are all right."

"I know," Fairbrother said. "And thank fuck they are."

With no time to question Fairbrother, Denzell said, "You need to get in here now. Fuck knows what's going on, and I don't know who's minding the bloody lads."

Denzell's stomach churned at the thought of Isaac left unguarded. He hadn't been able to see if the men who usually stood guard in the corridor were amongst those in the jostling crowd.

If anything happens to Isaac...

Fairbrother gave a shrill whistle through his teeth. It pierced the air, sharp and loud, and several coppers ran from the darkness towards the house. Denzell went back inside, thankful the heavy footsteps of the police thudded behind him.

"In there!" Denzell pointed at The Viewing Room door.

Cricket would think he'd alerted security, and for now that suited Denzell. But he was torn between helping in The Viewing Room and finding Isaac. Brotherly love won out. He dashed through the front doorway then rushed down the steps. Briggs and Oliver were running full pelt towards the side of the house where the car park was, adrenaline helping them along the way despite their injuries.

"Wait! Where are you fucking going?" Denzell chased after them.

"The lads," Briggs shouted. "We've got to save the lads! The door to get to them inside is blocked by them lot fighting."

221

"Fuck!" Speeding up, Denzell came abreast of them.

"Yeah." Oliver panted. "What if they're not guarded? What if the police don't get to them? D'you want your brother getting hurt? And Briggs *is* the police."

"What?" Denzell was staggered but couldn't sort through that information just yet.

He streaked across the car park until they all reached a side door. Denzell peered through the glass, relieved one of Cricket's men stood outside the mirror-room door and one outside the holding room.

"They're all right," Denzell gasped out.

He mentally worked out why the police hadn't come through the bottom door yet from The Viewing Room. There were enough of them, and he had no doubt some of them who'd been guarding the back of the house would have gone round to the front by now. Some would stay behind to make sure no one ran, and others still would enter the house and search out the rest of Cricket's men, but tonight there was only a skeleton crew, seeing as the viewings always ran so smoothly. Cricket had been proud to relate that fact.

That information had shocked Denzell this afternoon. He'd wanted all of Cricket's men caught, but the others wouldn't be back until morning, and unless Cricket had alerted them via his speed dial warning, the police would have to wait for their return.

The door at the other end of the corridor burst open, and the police poured through. Cricket's two men put up a good fight but were knocked to the floor in short order, handcuffed, then dragged into The Viewing Room.

Half of the police officers poured into the holding room.

On instinct, Denzell tried the outside door handle. It turned.

"Jesus! They left the fucking door *unlocked!*" He dashed inside and headed for the commotion at the other end. "Guard the fucking door!" he shouted over his shoulder.

Despite the high police presence, he managed to infiltrate the crowd, following Fairbrother inside the mirror room. He hoped, by the amount of time that had passed, that Isaac would be in there by now. He had to make sure his brother was all right, to see him one last time before being arrested and carted off.

Denzell stopped dead in the doorway. A lad, the one who'd refused to tell him his name despite his best efforts, stared at Fairbrother, a broad grin across his flushed face.

"I *knew* you'd come," he said. "I knew it!"

He flung himself at Fairbrother, who wrapped his arms around that slender back and held on tight.

"Jesus fucking Christ," Fairbrother said, his voice hoarse. "I had no fucking idea, son. No fucking idea you were here. I thought you'd just gone. That you'd buggered off once you were old enough."

Son?

Fairbrother drew back, holding the lad by the arms. "Let me look at you. Oh Jesus. It's so good to see you." He hugged him again, his son's cheek pressed to his chest.

The lad stared at Denzell. "Dad. That's one of them." He pulled away a little and pointed at Denzell.

Denzell's heart sank. "You all right, mate?" He took a step farther into the room.

"It's okay," Fairbrother said. "It's all right. Denzell's a good bloke."

"What?" The lad cocked his head.

"Did he hurt you?" Fairbrother asked.

"No, he...he was nice. Fed me. Talked to me. Made sure I was always okay."

"That's because he's the one who brought me here. Do you understand? He told me about this place. *He's* the one who saved you all."

Denzell's emotions spilled over, and a relieved sob barked from his mouth. "It's fine, mate," he choked out. "Everything's going to be fine. I told you that, didn't I, eh?"

Backing out of the room, his vision blurring, he stumbled past two policemen then pushed open the holding room door. The lads were all crying, some silently, some with great racking sobs, and Denzell sought out Isaac, dying to see him, dying to make sure he was okay.

He spotted him in a corner being checked over by a policeman. At Denzell's approach, Isaac widened his eyes and smiled through the tears.

He said, "The others told me… We weren't being adopted like you said. They said… But it's all right, because the police are here. Tell them not to let me go back home. Tell them, please. I can't go back there."

"You're not going home," Fairbrother said behind him. "Not to your parents' place anyway."

Denzell turned his head to look at Fairbrother, who stood in the doorway, his son glued to his side. Denzell mouthed "Thank you" and tried to hold his tears back. He failed. They spilled, a hot and steady stream, and he let them have their way. It had been a long, hard six months, and now he'd face the consequences of his part in this shit.

"Hopefully…" Fairbrother stepped closer. "You'll be living with your brother."

Denzell stared at Isaac.

"You've found him?" Isaac gazed at Fairbrother.

"You're standing in front of him," Fairbrother said.

"What?" Isaac looked at Denzell.

"Yes, mate," Denzell said, the words strained and tight. "It's me."

He couldn't manage to say anything else as his throat closed and emotion claimed him.

CHAPTER TWENTY-SEVEN

Cricket was marched from his house, greeted by the sight of Jeeps on his lawn. Their tyres had gouged great muddy swathes into the grass, and he gritted his teeth at the mess they'd made.

No fucking respect for other people's property, these security firms.

Shunted towards a Jeep, he memorised the license plate. After being shoved inside, he sat beside Jonathan and Kevin.

The door slammed shut, and the man stood guard.

"James Klein's been informed," Cricket said. "He'll take over until I get this mess sorted."

Jonathan nodded. "If we get nicked, like, if the security firm ring this in, what is it, Twenty years max?"

"Yeah." Cricket laughed heartily. "Ten for good behaviour."

"That's a long time, boss." Jonathan stared at the back of the seat in front.

"Yeah, it is if you intend serving it." Cricket smiled, content to sit in the Jeep while the firm sorted everything in the house.

"What do you mean?" Kevin frowned.

"Like I said, Klein's been informed. Speed dial warning—the wonders of modern technology. We're not even going to make it to the police station, if that's the way this goes—and if the fucking security team would just listen to who I am, none of this would be happening."

"Ah." Jonathan nodded.

"Thing is, I wanted Denzell with us." Cricket picked a speck of fibre off his trousers. "He'll enjoy Spain, I reckon."

"Yeah. He could do with getting a tan." Kevin chuckled.

Cricket sighed. "Let's just hope he gets put in here with us then, eh?" He took out his phone and selected the message option, punching in the registration number and: *Whoever is inside, get them to safety.*

He pressed SEND, prised out the SIM, then stamped the phone underfoot. He popped the SIM in his mouth and swallowed. All his contact numbers, gone. Klein used a burner and would ditch it the minute he'd finished organising what had to be done. They all used unregistered pay-as-you-go phones.

Cricket smiled smugly. "Your turn."

He'd instructed all his men to do this with their phones if they got caught or something out of the ordinary happened. He imagined the others doing so now as Jonathan and Kevin swallowed their SIMs.

"What about the others who weren't here tonight?" Jonathan asked.

"What about them? Klein will alert them."

The door swung open, and a security guard filled the space. In all the commotion, Cricket hadn't given a thought to being led outside by security people he'd hired.

Security people *Denzell* had hired.

"Fuck!" he growled. *That little fucking bastard!*

"Out!" the guard said, jerking his head.

Cricket allowed Jonathan and Kevin to leave first, giving himself time to work through the panic overtaking him. Denzell had betrayed him, probably knew all about Isaac being his brother, and now they were being ushered across the grass towards a van? A white one with a police stripe down the side.

Suddenly, twenty years didn't seem so funny.

CHAPTER TWENTY-EIGHT

Later, Denzell stood with Fairbrother, Briggs, Oliver, and some chief or other in Cricket's living room. He gained a warped sense of satisfaction that everyone had traipsed over the white carpet with their shoes on, dirtying it up. As the detectives talked—something about Briggs' undercover stint being over—Denzell's mind turned to Isaac. He'd been taken to the police station, where the doctor would check the lads over, and someone gently questioned them about their ordeal. The process could take days, or even weeks with counsellors used to dealing with people who'd suffered this kind of trauma.

They'd need extensive therapy, but Denzell hoped they'd all come through okay. He'd saved them a harsher incarceration while they'd been here and could only hope his kindness had gone some way to easing the psychological damage their torment had caused.

"You won't be going anywhere, will you, Denzell?" Fairbrother said.

Denzell faced him.

"As I was telling Chief Jones, you're not a threat," Fairbrother said. "You being here was under duress, and by helping those lads instead of helping Cricket, you've proved, at least to us, that you pose no threat to the public. You'll have to be questioned, no doubt about that, but I really don't see you need locking up. There'll be a trial, but I think your cooperation and behaviour towards the boys will hold you in good stead."

Relief left Denzell weak.

"Do you have somewhere you can stay?" Fairbrother asked. "Stupid question. Sorry. Would you like us to set you up somewhere? It might be advisable to move farther away. Who knows whether Cricket has contacts out there who might try to find you."

Denzell's stomach lurched. "Yeah. I see what you mean. Isaac...?"

Fairbrother smiled. "After he's been initially questioned and given support with experts in the field, we can arrange for him to come to you. Might be a couple of days. Mind you, seeing as Isaac was only here overnight, he probably won't need much medical attention—I think they only gave him lemonade in the cellar—but he *will* need counselling to help him understand the abuse he suffered at home wasn't his fault. Can you handle that and everything that goes with it?"

Denzell nodded, unable to say a word, the emotion of the moment too much.

CHAPTER TWENTY-NINE

Isaac sat in a room much like a lounge, in grey, loose tracksuit bottoms and a red T-shirt that was a little too big. He recalled the red coat he'd had out on the streets, and it brought Pete to mind and the nights they'd slept by the oil drum fire.

A woman sat opposite in a matching armchair, a clipboard on her lap. She looked kind, light wrinkles around her eyes, her auburn hair hanging in soft waves around her face. Her jeans and baggy jumper gave her a normal appearance, nothing like the counsellor she'd announced herself to be when she'd entered the room.

He'd expected a stern woman in a suit, hair pulled back so tight she looked startled.

"How are you, Isaac?" she asked.

"All right."

"Would you like to tell me about what happened? You don't have to yet, if it's too painful, but if you want to talk, I'll listen."

Her voice was one Isaac had imagined a proper mother's to be, and he warmed to her immediately. Words tumbled out quicker than he had time to form them, and he had to take a deep breath and slow down.

Once he'd finished, the woman smiled and nodded.

"I think you're going to be fine." She placed the clipboard on a coffee table between the chairs.

"I reckon so. Now I've found my brother." He frowned. "Can you get a message to someone for me?"

"Of course. Who would that be?"

"Pete."

"Pete who?"

"I don't know. He just told me his name was Pete."

"Is he a man from the house?"

"No. He's an old bloke I met when I left home. He looked after me."

"Do you know where I can find him?"

236

"Yeah. He sleeps under the bridge down by that disused car park off Moreland Road."

She picked up her clipboard and scribbled a few words. "What would you like me to tell him?"

"Just let him know the van took me, but I'm all right. That the police found me."

"Okay."

"He said he'd tell the police I'd been taken, see, and even if they didn't listen to him, I want him to think they did. I want him to think he saved me."

CHAPTER THIRTY

Two Weeks Later

Langham smiled at the sound of Oliver pottering about in the kitchen making dinner. That man had taken it upon himself to learn to cook well, and Langham wondered if it was them being so hungry after their ordeal, having gone without food for their duration at Cricket's, that had prompted him to appreciate their meals.

Langham appreciated many things now.

Being alive was one of them.

He walked into the kitchen. Leant on the doorjamb, gritting his teeth at the sharp pain from one of his healing welts. The skin was tight around the affected area. Antibiotics had cleared up any infection before it had the chance to infest his body, but it seemed his muscles and skin had had a tough time getting better until the last day or so. It would take a while for the scars to heal.

He studied Oliver, who was unaware he was being watched, iPod headphones jammed in his ears. He quick-fried some chicken breasts on the hob ready for them to be popped in the slow cooker in a spicy curry sauce of his own making, so he'd said, but an empty sauce jar peeked out of the bin.

Langham smiled, thinking back to others curries they'd had in this flat, nights spent talking about cases.

The mid-morning sun slanted though the vertical blinds covering the kitchen window.

Langham thought about the incidents that had led them to this moment—not in too much detail, mind, just the quick dash of a memory that he quickly squashed. They'd beaten the odds so far. And he thought about spirit, abandoning them in their time of need.

We could have done with them helping us, but where were they when we needed them?

They hadn't discussed their time in the cellar where they'd contacted each other through their minds. Langham hadn't really been able to get his head around Oliver's abilities, so for them to have finally connected in a way millions of others couldn't, it had thrown him.

"You still bothered?" Oliver asked.

"What about?"

"You know, that thing in the cellar. When we saw the same things while we were hanging there, that dream. You scared of what it means?"

Did he just read my fucking mind? "It freaked me out, I must admit." Langham laughed. "But I'll also admit that in the past I felt a bit naffed off you weren't able to connect with me in that way. And now you can so..." He shrugged. "We'll get through it. It's a case of having to, isn't it?"

"Yeah. Might not happen again anyway." Oliver smiled. "It was different at Cricket's, more stressful. We didn't have backup. You probably thought no one knew where we were, that Fairbrother wouldn't find us, so needed to connect with me instead."

The mention of Fairbrother brought to mind the fact that his son had been one of the young men. Shit, that had to have been difficult for Fairbrother, going to work every day and not being able to locate his own kid. Never talking about it, just turning up on the job every day and hiding his emotions, thinking his son had just upped and left one day for no apparent reason.

Were all coppers tough as nails?

"I've had nightmares about The Viewing Room," Oliver said. "The lads beneath the spotlight, crying and clawing at the mirror. I can't get to grips with the mentality of the customers, how some of them, when questioned, claimed it wasn't their fault they felt that way towards young men. It was 'just the way they were made'. If I live to be one hundred, I'll never understand the mad bastards."

"Me neither."

Langham had formed a bond with Denzell and Isaac since that terrible ordeal, meeting up a couple of nights at a family pub called The Lightning Bolt. Most of the lads had been returned to worried parents, but a couple had been taken into care. Their parents were either unfit to look after them, didn't give a shit they'd even gone missing in the first place, or couldn't be found. It was a fucking sorry business all round, and poor Oliver had been exposed to more of the realities of life—ones that lived and breathed right under his nose if only he'd taken the time to notice.

But you don't, do you? You get on, waking each day to deal with the shit in your own life, and what anyone else is doing is irrelevant. Until it involves you, then you're brought up short by the disgusting way some people behave. They should be caged, the lot of them, locked away.

"So," Langham said on a sigh. "Tomorrow I go back to work. Be weird, seeing as I've had the past two weeks off."

"At least we're alive, eh?"

Langham nodded. "That's something to be grateful for. I thought... When we were hanging in the cellar..."

Oliver frowned. "What about it?"

"I thought we were dead."

They were silent for a while.

Then Langham said, "We'll take each day as it comes. And if, later on, we need to speak to someone about this crap, well, we'll cross that bridge when we come to it. No harm in seeing a therapist, is there. If it means working through it and living without all that shit in our heads, it's worth a try." He could hardly believe he'd said that, seeing as at the start of his time undercover, he'd decided against it.

"So, for now we just go on as usual, yeah?" Oliver asked.

Langham nodded. "Yep. Time to move on."

"It is." Oliver blew out a long breath. "I suppose I'd better put the rice on then."

"Yeah. Boil in the bag by any chance?" Langham smiled.

"Well, yeah. May as well use that up."

"Whatever you say, mate. Teaching yourself to cook properly my arse."

Printed in Great Britain
by Amazon

47611714R00142